T0197182

CRY MY COUNTRY

MARK DIXON

BALBOA.
PRESS
A DIVISION OF HAY HOUSE

Balboa Press books may be ordered through booksellers or by contacting:

Balboa Press
A Division of Hay House
1663 Liberty Drive
Bloomington, IN 47403
www.balboapress.com.au
1 (877) 407-4847

Print information available on the last page.

ISBN: 978-1-5043-0151-0 (sc)
ISBN: 978-1-5043-0152-7 (e)

Balboa Press rev. date: 03/10/2016

Prologue

By the late 1970s the country known as Rhodesia was on its knees, economically and socially. It had become an international pariah through policies which kept its majority Black population without franchise and earning, on average, just ten per cent of White salaries.

Rhodesia's greatest ally, South Africa, itself in the middle of the horrendous apartheid period, was buckling to international pressure and distancing itself from the beleaguered, landlocked country.

Mozambique, to the east, had achieved independence in 1975 and become a haven for guerrilla fighters pledged to overthrow the Rhodesian regime.

International embargoes stripped the economic life from Rhodesia. No longer was it the shining success story of Africa. Every day life became a battle to survive. Terrorist strikes were frequent, particularly on isolated farms, but the militant action steadily grew closer to the main population centres, including the capital, Salisbury.

When, in 1978, guerrillas fired incendiary grenades and rockets into the country's main oil storage facility on outskirts of Salisbury, the fire burned for five days and in an instant destroyed Rhodesia's reserves. That came as two passenger aircraft were shot down, a move which had been described as breaking the Rhodesian will to persist.

But still the war continued. It was a nasty, bloody battle with each side committing atrocities in the name of freedom. One of the ugliest bush wars in Africa to that time, it far eclipsed other horrors further to the north, particularly in white Kenya's confrontation with the Mau Mau.

By 1979 the war had intensified into a grim horror story. That Rhodesia was doomed was a concept rejected by most White citizens. That Zimbabwe would be born from the ashes of the destruction was the core belief of those Black fighters and politicians pitted against them.

It is against that backdrop this story takes place.

Chapter One

Two shots rang out through the gloomy, rain-splattered bush. Both hit their mark and two terrorists were down, dead as they fell.

The M16, set on single fire, is a remarkable accurate weapon and both men using them were expert marksmen. Two more to the list. Shifting their weapons to three-shot fire, they shot at the few remaining dissidents who were fast disappearing into the storm. Maybe one more down, but too far away to tell for certain.

They then came in from the bush, from up near the Zambezi River, where they had been patrolling for two weeks.

Two weeks of mud and slush, the wet season had started and so neither Angus nor Daniel were too fussed about the call on the radio ordering them back to base immediately. If not sooner, the Boss had said.

In those two weeks they'd had five contacts with the terrs. Seven now were confirmed dead, several limping, bleeding, away into the bush. Not followed up, because with just two of them the risk of ambush was just too high, absolutely not worth the risk.

Also, they were stuffed. It had been four years in the army so far, most of the time chasing elusive shadows in the bush, hunting down the terrs, those terrorists who threatened Rhodesia with their new brand of democracy.

Achieved, largely, it seemed to Angus, through terrorising otherwise peaceful people who just wanted to live a normal life, in little villages, growing enough to feed their family, with a few cows and a close-knit tribal system.

The terrorists were also responsible for increasingly violent and atrocious attacks on white-owned farms. Dead of the night stuff, gangs of them surrounding farm houses, cutting the boundary wires, using RPGs, AK's and machetes to gruesome effect.

So the call on the scheduled check-in on the radio came as a bit of a relief. What puzzled Angus, however, was the degree of urgency in the Boss's voice. "Get back in ASAP," he'd said. "No fucking around."

They were now just a few hours away from the base, which in reality was just a collection of thrown-together huts, miles from nowhere, but at least with a working kitchen and showers, which if stoked properly, could be hot.

But in the meantime it was pissing with rain. Angus and Daniel had hardly spoken a word to each other for the past two weeks, which was standard operating procedure. Hand signals, a meaningful glance was all they really needed together at those sorts of times. They had, after all, known each other all their lives, literally born on the same day 25 years before.

Angus was white, Daniel was black. To them it meant nothing. For others, less racially tolerant, Angus was (behind his back) a kaffir-lover. To Angus, that was water off the duck's back. He shivered as another pelting of rain soaked them yet again. Daniel, born black, had worn the insults all his life. And now, serving in the Rhodesian military, as a black man, he couldn't, quite frankly, give a baboon's backside.

The forward base emerged through the gloom. A miserable mudhole. But better than trying to snatch some sleep sharing a blanket under the scarce cover of a tree. Almost like home, although home was 1000 km to the south.

There was a sentry trying his best to keep dry and warm and failing miserably on both counts. But he was awake sufficiently to challenge the mud-soaked scarecrows who came to the entrance of the perimeter wire. What precisely he had in mind remained right there as Angus and Daniel simply sidestepped him and walked toward the command post.

"Jesus....." Colonel John Wright said as they slid into his small, very pokey office which contained very little except for maps and a worn desk. "A bit wet out there?" He wasn't a bad bloke, Angus had decided long ago. Bit of a sense of humour, cut the leeway when he could and had an unabated dislike of red tape. Plus, being stuck as the CO in a shithole like Forward Base Zero rated as much fun as wiping your arse with a cactus.

"New orders," Wright said. "Effective immediately. There's a convoy leaving in 15 minutes and you're both on it. To Salisbury, where you will report straight away to Brigadier Johnson."

Angus blinked, as much to get the red mud from his eyelids as to catch the meaning of the order. He knew better than to ask why, although the question first and foremost in his mind remained "what the ..."?

"There're six trucks in the convoy. We've reserved a seat for you in the last one. Get your gear and get on it...we'll send the rest of your kit down later," Wright continued, face grim and lowering his eyes. After all, it wasn't every day that your two best special service men were promptly ordered back to the capital. But the Brigadier had spoken. His exact words: "Dunrow and Nkumo back here now. First thing." There was no arguing with that sort of order.

Wright shook himself and allowed a look into Angus and Daniel's eyes. "Sorry you're going. I don't know what's going down. But I do know you're not in the shit. It sounds like something's brewing and they need you both for whatever that may be."

He came around the table and shook the hands of Captain Angus Dunrow and Sergeant Daniel Nkumo. "Thanks men... you've both made life a bit easier around here."

Angus suddenly, totally irrationally, felt a tinge of nostalgia for Forward Base Zero. Yes, it was a shithole. But it, for the past three months, had been *their* shithole. He nodded at Wright, which involved a slight bending of his shoulders, because at his

6'5 versus Wright's 5'8 meant a bit of vertical leeway had to be granted.

"The last truck, sir?" he enquired. In a convoy the first and the last trucks were favourite terr targets. Knock the first off in the ambush, the last as well and the rest were bottled in, ripe for the plucking.

"Last one," Wright confirmed, then as if he had read Angus' mind: "All the rest are full...our civvies in uniform are heading home." Every man under the age of 60 had to do their military duty, usually four weeks a year, when they left comfortable jobs and comfortable lifestyles to battle it out with the terr invasion. Civvies in uniform. Very few enjoyed it, most made it clear they would rather be anywhere else. And Forward Base Zero was hardly a plum posting. Angus, despite his fatigue, felt a slight glow of enthusiasm creep back into his system. Without glancing at Daniel, he knew the big black man would feel the same. The chance to get away from prowling the Zambezi river border which linked the country to Zambia, to the north, hunting down and culling terrs, many of them just kids, could be the tonic he had been looking for inside, and failing to find, for months now.

He reached out and tapped the Colonel, John Wright, on the shoulder. "For a colonel, you're okay in my book, man," he smiled.

Wright looked momentarily abashed. Then he grinned.

Which was a very rare occurrence in the day of John Wright, who was totally fed up with bullshit orders and sending casualty reports through to Salisbury headquarters.

"Get on that truck," he said. He glanced at his watch. "You now have five minutes exactly before it leaves."

* * *

THE last truck was packed with civvies in uniform. They'd spread themselves out to be nice and comfortable. It was 300 km to Salisbury, the first 50 km over a diabolically slippery red mud road, with plenty of slow points where ambushes had and continued to occur.

Angus and Daniel hoisted their sodden packs over the tailgate and motioned for the rest to move up towards the front of the truck. There were muted mumblings and grumblings, but once the 15 others saw both the size and the condition the new men were in there was no room for argument. Angus and Daniel sat adjacent to each other, on either side of the rear opening. Angus was right-handed, Daniel left, so it was an easy matter for them to cover the rear with their M16s.

Any ambush would start with a warning, the first truck in the convoy being hit. Then, Angus knew, the first of the terr ambushes, or in this case the last, would open fire on the rear truck. Probably with RPGs, rocket-propelled grenades.

They scrunched into as a comfortable position as possible, both shivering from the cold.

"Thought you might like this," a booming voice came over the tailgate as Sergeant Ben Hill loomed from the dusk. He passed up a small canvas holdall and winked at Angus. "To ward off the chills," he explained. Angus grinned. Hill was a good man, the base's Mr Fixit, who could be relied on to scrounge the most unlikely items. The bag felt light, but there was a faint tinkling noise coming from within. As Angus opened the holdall, he found there were two blankets...and two bottles of the fiery, gut-warming Cape Brandy.

"One of these days I owe you the best steak dinner in Rhodesia," Angus said to Hill. Hill winked again and turned away. In less than two minutes the convey lurched into motion, at first slipping and sliding with the growl of over-revved engines, then settling into a slow, but reasonably comfortable pace.

The returning troops inched further away from Angus and Daniel. Not just because of their appearance, Angus reflected. They must have also stunk to high heaven. For a moment he thought of wallowing in a steaming hot bath in Salisbury, then shook his head. Later. First get through the 50 km of slop and mud. He looked at Daniel, who as always looked imperturbable. The dark face a mask, the steady brown eyes unreadable.

Angus grinned to himself. His own face was as dark as Daniel's, with the camouflage cream, the filth and the dirt. They could be twins, he thought.

The 50 km trip took more than two hours as the trucks ground along. Either the terrs were having a night off, or, more likely were off hunting easier game than six trucks with heavily armed soldiers aboard.

As they reached the tarmac road there was visible relief all round. The convoy lifted speed and the kilometres began to speed by. Angus reached into the holdall and extracted the Cape Brandy. He passed it to Daniel, who grinned and took a hefty belt before returning the bottle. Angus was more circumspect, just enough to get the inner fire started and warm up his body, which despite the blanket wrapped around him was starting to ache with cold, rain and the two-week tab in the bush. He also had a long-held respect for Daniel's ability to hold alcohol. He'd seen the man, as a boy of fourteen, drink most of a bottle of brandy, then steady as a rock, shoot a gemsbok from four hundred yards.

He passed the bottle back to Daniel. "Have another, pisshead," he grinned. Daniel smiled back and obliged. Whatever the troopies in the front of the truck thought of the situation, they weren't saying.

Just 100 km from Salisbury the convoy came across a military roadblock. No ordinary one, either. The trucks were diverted into a large, bare patch cut from the bush, surrounded by barbed wire and lit with blazing arc lights. At least 50 armed MPs were standing in dual formation, as the convoy was directed into a corridor between them.

"What the hell is this?" Daniel asked one of the troopies. The man grimaced. "New regulations..we get searched on the way home to make sure we haven't pinched any stuff from the forward base."

*   *   *

Chapter Two

"Pinched any stuff," Angus laughed. "Such as what? Mud?"

A voice over a foghorn barked orders. "All men off the trucks and bring all kit with you." The troopies slowly obeyed, cursing while gathering kitbags and weapons and dismounting, forming a line in front of the MPs.

Angus and Daniel stayed where they were. Not their problem. One of the benefits of the special forces was the exemption from pinheads trying to asset authority over them.

One by one the MPs went through the kit the men had managed to bring back from Base Station Zero. As was expected, there was nothing illicit. Just mud and exhausted men.

Angus and Daniel waited patiently, it was after all, none of their business. Until a bristling lieutenant, fresh from school, Angus judged, decided to check the trucks. He came to the last one, where Angus and Daniel were finishing the last of the brandy and sharing a cigarette.

A bantam rooster, Angus immediately decided. Strutting with new-found authority. Ramrod straight, an appearance of a moustache on his thin upper lip.

"Did you men not hear the order?" he barked at Angus and Daniel. "All men off the trucks for inspection."

Angus looked down at him. Then glanced at Daniel. In accord, they vaulted from the back of the truck and looked down at the bantam rooster. "You are...?" Angus inquired, in a deceptively moderate tone. The bantam looked slightly taken aback. Both men were dishelleved, filthy in fact. Both towered above him. And neither looked in the least perturbed by his new lieutenants' bars, nestled on his shoulders.

"Lieutenant Godfrey Ryan, Military Police," he snapped. "You are now required to undergo a body search and identify yourselves. I also demand an explanation as to why you disobeyed a direct order to disembark from the truck."

Daniel smiled to Angus. "I think I need a piss," he said. Angus nodded in concurrence. They walked together around the bantam and relieved themselves against a nearby tree.

"Radio Salisbury SAS HQ if you have any problems with our ID," Angus said. Normally, he would have just told the the little man to mind his own peace. "Now," as he buttoned his fly. "Fuck off."

Lieutenant Godfrey Ryan went a lighter shade of pale. With the Selous Scouts, the SAS, the Special Air Services Regiment, were the most feared of all the anti-terrorists military forces in the country. He attempted to rise another half an inch or two in height so to regain some pride, but Angus and Daniel had simply walked around him and were back in the truck.

The convoy rolled into Salisbury just as dawn was beginning to break, the early morning glow on the jacaranda-lined streets creating an illusion of peace which was far from coming in the troubled country.

The first five trucks kept moving, to the base where the troopies would be debriefed and allowed to return to their creature comforts. Hot baths and welcoming wives, Angus wryly thought. The last truck, theirs, stopped at the front gate to the SAS headquarters. Angus and Daniel gathered their packs and weapons and disembarked. Angus looked back into the truck and nodded at the remaining men. "Good luck," he said.

They walked to the barricaded entrance gate, where two sentries were waiting, watching the two filthy apparitions appear in the dawn light. "Dunrow and Nkumo," Angus explained. The senior sentry nodded. "We were told to expect you," he said. He glanced at his watch. "The Brig is waiting."

That came as no surprise to either Angus or Daniel. Brigadier Harry Johnson was a notorious insomniac and slept in snatches during brief periods he managed to grab during the day and night.

They trudged the 500 metres into the main camp and walked to the Brig's office, a highly functional but austere building. But it was from this office the Brig co-ordinated 500 SAS personnel thoughout Rhodesia. And outside the country as well, on highly-classified clandestine incursions into neighbouring Zambia, Botswana and Mozambique.

Even though the sun was now starting to make inroads heralding a hot day ahead, there was still a slight mist around the camp. Some early risers were pounding the pavement, exercising already well-tuned muscles for missions ahead.

And in the Brig's front office, Corporal Lance van de Mer was at his station, clean, crisp and almost overwhelming efficient. With the Brig as his direct boss, he was in constant demand at any time. But van de Mer complained little. It did, after all, beat the daylights out of being out in the bush. Like the two apparitions who walked through the door.

"Jesus...," he started to comment on the general state of appearance of Angus and Daniel. Then thought better of it. "He's waiting in there," pointing to the door of the Brig's private domain. "Go straight in."

Angus and Daniel lowered their bergens to the ground and stacked their weapons carefully before walking through the door. The Brig looked up from a large scale map he'd been perusing and immediately stood. He was, in Angus' eyes, about 50, but every mission he had planned and co-ordinated was etched into the lines around his eyes and forehead.

He crossed around the desk and shook first Daniel, then Angus' hands. He then sniffed. "God almighty. Haven't you boys heard of showers? Open the windows for heaven's sake." But there was humour in the deep blue eyes and a slight smile on his face.

"Well done on that last job. It's been confirmed that one of the five you culled was one of the biggies. Excellent Ndele himself. God knows what he was doing this side of the border. Normally confines himself to a nice safe place in Zambia. Well done."

Angus nodded. He suspected their sudden recall had very little to do with taking out another terr. And was almost instantly proved right.

"We have new plans," the Brig said. "Detailed briefing back here at 0900." He glanced at his watch. "That gives you two hours to clean up. So," he sniffed again. "You'd better get a move on."

Chapter Three

"We're changing the strategy," Brigadier Johnson said. "Effective immediately." He carried on without pause, stone cold eyes switching alternatively from Angus to Daniel and back. The effect, Angus thought was quite mesmerising. The Brig was an imposing character with a disposition which could change, as if by whimsy from vast warmth to icy cold. But Angus knew there was nothing whimsical about Johnson. He was a man of immense self-control and also, Angus had long decided, a superb actor capable of changing scripts mid-scene.

"You're both from Matabeleland. You are both fluent in Sindebele. You both know the land, the people, the history, and the issues."

Which was rather a superfluous statement, Angus thought. Of course Daniel spoke Sindebele, the language of the Ndebele people who lived in the south of Rhodesia, in Matabeleland, and were directly descended from the Zulu people of Southern Africa. Daniel, after all, was Matabele. Angus had learned the language from the time he first learned English. And yes, they both knew the land. The Dunrow family was one of the largest landholders in the lush land just to the south of Bulawayo, Rhodesia's second capital. And Daniel's family held the rights to an adjacent farm, leased on peppercorn rent from Angus' father.

He waited silently for the Brig to get to the point. Which would not be too far away, he knew. Johnson rarely wasted words.

"Yet you are posted in the outskirts of Shona land," the Brig expanded. The Shona, the dominant tribe in Rhodesia by numbers, claimed the northern part of Rhodesia. Matabele and Shona generally despised each other. Traditionally, before the arrival of Cecil Rhodes and his columns of armed white men and grandiose ideas for the new country which would bear his name, Matabele traditionally slaughtered Shona at will, regarding them as far lesser beings in the overall scheme of matters.

That had changed with the advent of white colonialism, but the animosity remained. Indeed, both Shona and Matabele dissidents had separate armies fighting the Rhodesians in their liberation struggle, Robert Mugabe's Shona ZINLA and Joshua Nkomo's Matabele ZAPRA.

Angus almost shrugged. This was hardly news and definitely not worth the rush back to Salisbury for what was starting to amount as a history lesson.

"So," the Brig abruptly snapped. "All Matabeleland special forces are returning to Matabeleland. Shonaland special forces vice versa." He leant forward to emphasise the point. "This time it's going to be different. We want you out there, in the land you know and the people you know, being highly aggressive."

Which made sense so far, Angus thought, if about four years' overdue. He kept silent. There would be more, of that he was sure. The Brig didn't disappoint him.

"Within the Bulawayo-based SAS we're forming a new, elite group. All totally familiar with the area, all able, at a pinch, to pass themselves off as terrs." He nodded at Daniel. "That won't be difficult for you. Angus might have to hide in the bushes nearby and listen."

He paused. "We want action; we want to know where the bastards are going to strike next. And...most importantly, we want them taken care of before any action goes ahead. Pre-emptive action, gentlemen. Follow-ups across the borders are authorised at your discretion." He nodded as Angus.

Angus suddenly came wide awake. Here was something he hadn't anticipated. At my discretion? What the hell did that mean?

"Sir...," he began, but was chopped off by Brigadier Johnson. "You will be the leader of the new team. Well...." he stopped for an instant. "There is a colonel in charge of the logistics, based back in Bulawayo. You'll liaise with him so closely you'll be brothers. But you are in charge of operational decisions. That is on the ground, in the bush, in your element. Your initial squad is 50 men. You choose them, you make them into the most feared unit in Matabeleland."

Angus interrupted at last, stunned by the enormity of the proposal. "The Selous Scouts, sir?" he inquired. The Scouts were regarded as the best in the business when it came down to deep-bush work, surveillance, interception and gathering the intelligence which was utilised to mount deadly counter-attacks. It was widely accepted the Scouts had contributed to more than 70 per cent of all terr fatalities.

There was strong rivalry between the Selous Scouts, many of whom had been former SAS and the SAS itself. But it was also a rivalry based on mutual respect.

"Listen to me," Johnson snapped. "I said we are forming an aggressive, on the ground and very deadly force. You will act together as a unit, and act with utmost ruthlessness." Angus almost shivered. Instead he gathered his thoughts. A small, highly mobile force with authority from the top to chase down terrorists, hunt them out and perhaps put a dent into the flood of dissidents coming across the borders. It was certainly worth a try.

"Why me?" he instead asked. "And where does Daniel fit in?"

The Brig pieced him with the ice-eyes for just a moment. "Because currently you have four medals for bravery, including the Silver Star, you have years of experience, you have the right skill fits." Johnson then allowed himself a slight smile. "And your political connections aren't bad."

Angus inwardly groaned. Yes, his father was the Minister for Finance in the Ian Smith Government, plus occupying a seat on the Security Council. Prime Minister Ian Smith himself had been a frequent visitor to Hillview Farm in the earlier, less troubled times. But Angus had never, and never intended to, use his father's influence to get ahead in any field.

"Good," the Brig suddenly sat back; satisfied matters had been sorted, and then frowned for an instant. He looked to Daniel. "Forgive me Daniel. You will be Angus' right hand man. By the way," he suddenly smiled and reached into the top drawer of his desk, emerging with a small box which he handed to Daniel, then stood. Daniel and Angus instinctively followed him standing. The Brig saluted Daniel and held out his hand to the big man. "Congratulations Sergeant Major. This is long-overdue." He glanced at Angus. "You'll have to wait Dunrow. You've enough gongs for now." The Silver Cross was awarded for extreme valour in combat situations and Angus could have won it many times over so far.

Chapter Four

The last shots rang out through the bush as Angus and his team finished the job. He, Daniel and the other three, carefully selected for the special team, which Angus had decided to call Leopards, had lain in ambush for two days now, waiting for terrorists to come along the path. Terrorists hunted in the night, so too did Leopard squadron. The same path they had carefully avoided for fear on anti-personnel mines...and leaving tracks. Ten terrs had finally come along, distinguished by their ragged denims and their AK47 weapons. All were now post-history. Stealth, aggression and take no prisoners had been the order. So far the Leopards were gaining an awesome reputation, among those in the know, for all three.

But they were tired, filthy and almost out of ammunition. Time to rest, Angus decided, and once they had frisked the bodies of the dead terrs for any papers of significance, and finding none, he gave the word. Many of the terrs were almost illiterate and occasionally orders were written in large English print. The orders could hold the names of friendly villages where food and shelter could be obtained, rendeavou points for meeting other patrols and the names of targets, which were mostly farms in outlying areas.

"Time to go," he said to his men. "Back to the truck." Their transport had been carefully hidden twelve days before, but was still a full day's trek back. About twenty miles, Angus estimated, taking into consideration the scrub they would work their way though. "Think of that first cold beer," he said with a grin.

And thinking of the cold beer, he inwardly smiled at the memory of the train trip from Salisbury to Bulawayo, an overnight journey where he and Daniel had shared a first-class cabin. With a case of beer and a bottle of gin. They also lugged their own special carrying case, a large trunk containing the best of the AK47's he and Daniel had collected over the previous four years. None were original; all had been stripped and rebuilt with various parts from other AK's turned into products which could have come directly from the factory.

There had been a bit of consternation at the Salisbury train station. A hundred or so drafted soldiers were being ordered onto the train, taking allocated seats to the rear, ordered abruptly and loudly by a pompous major. Angus and Daniel simply ignored him and boarded the train, finding their first-class cabin. And settled in, the first cold bottle of beer already opened. Until the irate major burst into their cabin, which they had left unlocked.

"When I give an order, I expect to be obeyed instantly," he snarled. Then he looked at the pair, who had not even troubled themselves to stand. "Ah...not in my mob, are you?" Angus just looked at the man without interest. His tolerance of bureaucracy had reached its lowest level ever, not that it had been especially high from the beginning. The major blinked, then cast his eyes around the cabin, then backed away out of the door way. "Sorry to trouble you," he muttered.

"And there," Angus said to Daniel "goes the last of the true warriors". Daniel grinned and clinked bottles with Angus. "Wasn't it you who told me sarcasm is the lowest form of wit?"

*   *   *

It took slightly less than a day to reach their truck, covered with camouflage cloth and well hidden in the bush, but still the Leopard team of four had painstakingly checked for booby traps. Finally satisfied, they started the engine and headed for the five hour drive to Bulawayo. Angus had been on the radio to HQ, told them of their progress and intentions to head back to base.

To his amazement, the Colonel had replied: "Take a week off for you and Daniel. You need it." Angus hadn't argued. Yep, they needed it. And the HillView farm was just a 15 minute drive from the small township of Mbelo, where there was a good drinking house, co-incidentally owned by the Dunrow family.

"New orders," he informed the Leopards. "Daniel and I are getting off in Mbelo. At the colonel's orders. Now, my orders to you are that you will join Daniel and me for more than a couple of beers." Four dusty hours later, they finally hit the tarmac road and motored into Mbelo. Pulling around the back of the drinking hole, which overlooked a small river and had lush green grass and tables set outside for the more posh and discerning drinkers, as opposed to the dedicated drunks and brawlers who frequented the front bar facing the only road through Mbelo, the Leopards settled themselves at a convenient table under the shade of a Mopani tree.

Jurgen, the pub's manager was delighted to see them. Originally from South Africa, he had come to Rhodesia seeking his fortune chasing elusive diamonds, but luck had deserted him in that regard. But he did consider himself lucky to have landed the manager job after a chance meeting with Angus's father in Salisbury. A massive man, Jurgen had no trouble with the front bar brawlers, but also knew how to charm the more elite who chose to wine and dine at the Colonial Inn.

His greeting was more than outwardly effusive. He held the Dunrow family, and Angus in particular, in high regard. Angus, after all, had played cricket in between army time, for the Rhodesian national team which competed in the South African Currie Cup. And had scored a couple of flawless centuries. Jurgen loved cricked more than his wife, which was fortunate, considering he was now on wife number four. A player, not a stayer, he had once told Angus. And unlike many of his countrymen, and many of Angus' own white Rhodesians, he had no colour problems. Daniel, again, was a man he admired. And Daniel's sister, Sally, a nurse at the Bulawayo Hospital, was especially admired...though from a safe distance.

"Gentlemen," he began. "Beer?" A nod from Angus. "And food?" That earned another nod, with a tired smile. "Thanks, Jurgen," he said. "And keep them coming."

It was late that afternoon when Angus finally reached HillView Farm, after first dropping Daniel off at his adjacent property, which Daniel shared with his sister, father and two younger siblings. Both of whom, although ten years younger showed every promise of becoming even more strapping than Daniel himself. Angus had borrowed one of the cars from Jurgen's extensive collection of old bombs which the publican had carefully and painstakingly restored.

He pulled into the extensive driveway to the HillView homestead, a grand settler-era edifice first constructed by Angus' grandfather and added to over the generations. Built from local quarried stone, with a wide stoep around the entire veranda, with now flowering jacaranda trees glowing purple in the afternoon sun, meticulously maintained by the staff of seven, the HillView house was only marred now by the high security fences built to deter potential terrorist attack.

Tired, filthy and just a little drunk, he opened the front door, to be greeted by Matilda, the matriarch of the servants. Matilda, he had known since being first born. Indeed, Matilda regarded herself as the head of the household and maintained strict discipline over the household affairs. Matilda was, as far as Angus could judge, nudging seventy, weighed a colossal amount, with enormous bosoms which Angus in his younger boyhood days had nestled into on many times in times of crisis...like the time he had been bitten by a scorpion when putting a boot on. Since that day he had learned the lesson – always shake them out first before inserting a foot.

Now, Matilda beamed and embraced Angus into her mammoth body. "Angie...her pet name for Angus ever since he was born...my boy." Angus had always been Matilda's favourite, the eldest son. His younger brother and sister, now studying in

South African universities, had also received her love, but Angus to her was a true Matabele, despite his colour.

"But," she continued in Sindabele, "You stink like a hyena. Go and wash and I'll feed you something to fill your rumbling stomach, which reminds me..."

Angus cut her off. Once Matilda started on recollections, it could last for hours. "Matilda, my favourite lady, please just pack me a basket and I'll go to the Pool." He knew that father and mother were both in Salisbury on government business and the Pool was his special place for relaxation. He and Daniel had created it, in their teen years, at the foot of the hill which gave HillView farm its name, digging out tons of rock and dirt where a small stream flowed down. They'd then dammed the drainage flow, resulting in a crystal clear swimming hole about the size of a tennis court. It was a private sanctuary, off limits to all staff on the HillView Farm and surround by beautiful native trees and flowers, fenced off at the outer limits to distray wildlife, such as leopards and lions from becoming too familiar with the place.

"Of course Angie," Matilda beamed once again, the giant smile displaying sparkling teeth of which a grand piano would boast. She backed away, theatrically holding her nose and barked an order to the kitchen staff. "Joseph will bring it to the stable for you."

She was correct in assuming that Angus would take Nelson, his favourite stallion for a long-overdue ride. Nelson would only accept Angus on his back. Other family members, including father Jonathon, had been unceremonaly dumped from the saddle the moment he attempted to mount. The same fate had been dealt to younger brother Thomas. Now Nelson roved in a large paddock near the homesite and would only come to a whistle from Angus... which he hadn't heard for far too long.

Angus placed two fingers in his mouth and emitted a piercing two-tone whistle which carried across the mile-long paddock. At first there was no reaction. Angus waited a minute, then repeated the whistle. He need not have bothered. Coming full tilt towards him was a huge black stallion, galloping and trembling at the same time, if that was at all possible. Nelson was one supercharged horse. And he hadn't been ridden for at least three months, passing the lonely days servicing the odd mare which had come into season, but even that novelty had worn off...Angus had once seriously considered joining the Greys' Scouts, where men very much like the Leopards operated on horseback, riding through the veldt in chase of the terrs.

But he liked the Leopard command too much, and, to be fair, Nelson was really a pet...he'd raised him from a newborn colt as his, not as a military horse. And as Nelson stormed to the stable fence, every fine muscle quivering with excitement, Angus knew he had made the right decision. He had many human friends, but very few equine ones, and of those Nelson was right up there as the best.

Nelson stood at least 17 hands, an imagery in black ebony, though going a bit soft from lack of exercise, Angus judged. He grinned as the huge stallion pig-rooted to a stop, just a handshake away from the stable fence. Nelson looked to him with huge brown eyes, full of adoration. Angus reached over and stroked the stallion's head, ears and nose, then, as if secretly, fed him a large mango. Of all Nelson's favourites', mangos were it. As a colt, the Dunrow family had to fence off their small mango experimental plantation to keep the bugger out. Even then, Nelson had foraged around the fence, hoping for titbits. Now, Nelson was in the horses' version of seventh heaven.

And his ecstasy grew higher when Angus opened the stable gate and brought out the riding gear...the halter, saddle and the gun holsters. Even on his own farm Angus carried two guns, the trusty M16 and a Remington shotgun.

Angus decided to give Nelson his head as he mounted and pointed him to the furthest point of the home paddock. Nelson responded with glee, galloping at a pace which took the distance in just a few minutes. The big horse was loving every second, and, Angus realised, so too was he. The power of the mighty beast under him, responding instantly to every command, avoiding potential problems of holes or just effortlessly hurdling fallen branches in the way was intoxicating. Twice they went around the huge paddock, Nelson and Angus both feeling younger with every stride. Eventually, they came to the fence at one side which divided the Dunrow property from the nearest neighbour to the south, the Hansen family. Angus was tempted to jump the fence and go and see the ruins of old Tom Hansen's house, old Tom himself having fallen victim to a terrorist raid two years' previously. He'd had just one child, a young daughter, from memory, Angus thought, about twenty now, who was studying nursing in South Africa and had been away at the time of the attack. But, he thought, enough grimness for a while.

So he decided against it. Time for Old Tom memories later. Time for a swim in the Pool now. He turned Nelson back toward the Pool. Only half a mile and Nelson had burned enough energy now to canter sedately to one of his favourite destinations. Although all but family were barred from the Pool, Nelson had special access rights, albeit unknown to the rest of the family. Nelson loved nothing better than a good dip in the Pool.

Also, Angus decided, he was absolutely stuffed. An hour or so near the Pool, a swim to get the worst of the sludge off him – although Nelson seemed to appreciate the advanced aroma coming from his master – and home in time for dinner. He knew Matilda would have prepared a homecoming dinner fit for a king. Although, he was sure in the picnic basket there would be enough provisions to feed half of Matabeleland.

Angus turned Nelson's head toward to Pool. Nelson seemed to sniff it, because the hair on the back on his main straightened. Nelson also gained another pace or two as he headed to his favourite place. There was no need for Angus to guide him. Nelson had it firmly in his mind exactly where he was going.

The big stallion's ears straightened and he found another ounce of energy as he raced to the fenced off area surrounding the Pool. But, as they approached, Angus sensed something was wrong this scenario. The hair on the back of his neck seemed to prickle. The cyclone fence around the area was intact, but the gate was ajar. He reined Nelson in, who though very reluctantly,

21

obeyed. Just before the gate, Angus dismounted and tied Nelson to the main fence, ignoring the implied hurt in Nelson's eyes.

"Just a moment, old chap," he whispered into the horse's ear. Angus took his rifle from the holster and cautiously approached the Pool. It was only a matter of 50 metres, through a well-worn trail. But experience dictated to Angus that trails were where mines were laid, so he moved gently through the bush.

As he passed through the last of the brushes and came upon the Pool, Angus had to hold his breath. There, start naked and as beautiful as the sunrise was a vision from heaven. Blonde, lithe, breasts to cry for and shaking the last of the drops of water from her hair, was the most delightful woman he had ever seen. Blazing blue eyes and a mouth which was made for kissing.

All of which Angus noticed in the two second she took to realise his presence.

"Get the fuck away from here," she screamed at Angus. And a colourful language to go with it, Angus appreciated. "You don't belong here, get away!" She rushed to her horse, a filly, and went to take what Angus thought might have been a gun.

"So sorry," he apologised. Although not for a moment stopping ogling the naked beautiful woman in front of him.

"I must have stumbled on the wrong place."

"Damn right you did," the woman replied. "We shoot people like you here."

Angus suddenly realised his appearance was far from reassuring. Filthy dirty after three weeks tabbing in the bush, still covered with camouflage cream, probably stinking to high heaven, even from the ten yards separating them. No prize from heaven, he guessed.

Wryly, he put his hands up. "Please don't shoot...I just want to go home."

He backed away into the bush, with his hands still theatrically in the air. Once back on the trail, he grinned and unleashed Nelson from the fence. A beautiful filly, with a beautiful filly, he judged. But somewhere in the back on his mind, he was sure he had met her before, maybe years ago.

"The swim will have to wait, Nelson," he told the stallion, who nodded his head as if he understood. "Home, mate." Nelson needed no further urging and with a lunge which could have unseated Angus, had he not been prepared for it, bolted in the direction of the stables.

The huge stallion loved nothing more than a full-out gallop and, even now, lathered with sweat, he reached full speed in just a few strides. Not for the first time, Angus wondered how Nelson would go in the Bulawayo races. Probably flatten any horse which dared come near him, he realised.

*   *   *

Matilda gave Angus a menacing grimace as he walked back into the homestead. "You haven't swum and you still stink like a hyena," she accused.

"Matilda my dear mother," using the Matabele phrase, which in no way inferred Matilda was his birth mother. "I was chased from the Pool by a lovely naked blonde. She thought I was a bandit and was prepared to shoot me on the spot."

Matilda, whose girth was only surpassed by her sense of humour, began chuckling, the fat on her face creasing, her huge bosom heaving and finally her legs giving way, till she had to sit on one of the couches. "Chased away by a naked woman?" With that, hilarity overcame her, until tears were rolling down her cheeks. "My brave warrior," she finally gasped.

Angus regained, very slowly, the little remaining dignity he retained and went outside, falling boots and all into the swimming pool. A brown sludge remained behind him as he ploughed through the laps. Finally, he rose from the pool and stripped naked. After all, there was nothing Matilda hadn't seen before. With a frosty composure, he strode through the house to his rooms. Matilda, he was annoyed to see, was still sitting on the couch, a discourse in blubbering ebony. She was thoroughly enjoying herself. By the time Angus reached his rooms, he began to see her point of view. Chased off his own property by a naked blonde? He began to chuckle too.

A quick shower, a neat shave and dressed in khaki shorts with a polo top, he ventured back to the rear of the house. Matilda, he was relieved to see, was back at her work station, ordering the rest of the home staff over the preparations for dinner. He walked over and put his arm around her massive shoulder.

"Pretty funny, I suppose," Angus whispered into her ear, lest any of the other staff overheard. "Do you have any idea who she is?" The image of the beautiful woman was first and foremost in his mind. But who the hell was she? A wildcat, that was for sure.

Matilda looked at him and suddenly lost her frivolity. "You remember Uncle Tom of course," she began. Angus nodded. Poor Uncle Tom, brutally murdered by a dozen attackers. "Her name is Kate and she is his daughter. Just back from nursing training in South Africa and wanted to see what the farm was like now."

Angus nodded; his family had immediately bought Uncle Tom's farm. Uncle Tom, as he was universally known throughout Matabeleland, and incorporated it into HillView. But Matilda hadn't finished. "She is best friends with Sally, they are now nursing together at the hospital in Bulawayo."

Angus felt like he had been hit on the head with a strong right hand punch. Sally, Daniel's sister, a statuesque Matabele lady who had overcome all odds, racism included to join the elite nursing team in the emergency department of the Bulawayo Hospital. He had known her from birth and between them more than friendship had grown.

If Daniel was his black brother, Sally was his black sister. Not for the first time, Angus reached into the depths of disgust he felt for the regime governing his country which segregated on the basis on race, on colour. Angus was colour-blind as far as people were concerned. Although in the interests of diplomacy, particularly as far as he father's political career was involved, he was also in the public eye a successful white farmer, employing more than a hundred black labourers. But he had few illusions about the concept of White Supremacy. His cynical side said there were as many white mongrels and black mongrels in the population – and vice versa. Sally was a rare jewel and Daniel was his best friend.

"Surely she's not staying at Uncle Tom's," he asked Matilda. The beaten up home was due for the bulldozer after the terrorist attack which had claimed the old man's life.

"No, Angie," Matilda softened as she saw the expression on Angus' face. "She lives at the nursing quarters and came here early this morning," and Matilda could for a moment not contain her natural humour. "Before you came home roaring drunk and stinking like a hyena. She said she would like to swim in the Pool."

"Where is she now?" Angus demanded. At the very least, an apology might soothe some of the way out of the situation. She was, after all, gorgeous. And spirited. And....Angus stopped his train of fantasy. A five second encounter, with someone running for their gun, did not relationships united make ... even if the glimpse he had seen of her had been the best thing he had seen in many a long week.

"Back in Bulawayo," Matilda offered, her heart softening more as she read Angus' mood. She had loved this boy since birth and now he was a big, strong man... and she had to admit a warrior in the Matabele class. But there was also sensitivity about Angus she loved. And, she secretly admitted, she was one of the few who was privy to that very private side to the man.

"But you will see her tomorrow," she continued. Angus stared blankly at her. "Garry Grace's wedding," she said. "You have been invited and now that you have come home, you must go." Angus inwardly groaned. He had determined not to be anywhere near the Grace nuptials, to a vacuous brunette of whom many of the eligible bachelors in Bulawayo had experienced her pleasures. But now, he suddenly looked forward to it. "She'll be there?" he demanded of Matilda. Matilda smiled. "Of course, Angie ... so I will make sure your uniform is spot-smart."

Chapter Five

The crowd at the wedding was boisterous, friends and family coming from miles around for the festivities. It was a welcome moment of respite, almost a return to the good old days when the wedding and its aftermath would be expected to last for at least the weekend. But now before dusk was the closing time; time to head back to the sanctuary of homes before night fell and the risk of terrorist ambush became reality.

So there was almost a frantic air of excitement by as early as ten in the morning, champagne already being served before the brief ceremony on the lawns of the Grace family farmhouse. The ceremony itself went according to plan, Gary managing the stumble through his few lines and Julie, his bride managing virginal simpers as she whispered her piece.

"And now, we sing a hymn of hope for the future," the priest announced. "The words are all in you Orders of Service." Angus glanced down. "Onward Christian Soldiers"...seemed a bloody funny choice for a marriage he blinked. But then Gary had always made some bloody funny choices...witness the bride, he thought. Around him, friends of Angus coughed nervously. What Angus lacked in musical tone, sense of rhythm or melody he made up for in spades with energy and volume.

As the first tentative words started to come from the congregation to the accompaniment of a wheezy old organ, played by the priest's dear old Aunt Grace, Angus came in four words too late. Although he was in the second furthest rank at the rear the bellow of a bull in the agony of ecstasy of mating with a cow overwhelmed the congregation. Startled heads at the front turned as they tried to match Angus' own special beat to the new look hymn. Oblivious, Angus carried on to the bitter end, totally unaware of his soldier friends turning puce in an effort not to laugh. Job done, he finished with a flourish which had the servants, many of whom had gathered from their assigned stations to wonder at this strange booming echoing across the veldt. Only ingrained manners and the fear of a white man obviously badly affected by the sun prevented them from breaking into wild applause. Angus beamed around proudly. He'd always liked a good hymn.

Then, almost like a gunshot start to a race, the party began in earnest. Champagne, whisky, beer and gin were complemented by barbequed Matabele-grown beef, slowly cooked to perfection over an open pit fire for the past three days. Angus was involved in war stories with some of his army chums, some of whom he hadn't seen for a year or more. They were severely punishing the beer supplies and the conversation was becoming increasingly raucous.

But from the corner of his eye he was transfixed by a vision of beauty. Tall, rounded in the right spots and all set off by glowing blonde hair which seemed to capture the sunlight and highlight her deep blue eyes. All set off by a stunning outfit which he decided could have only come from South Africa's latest fashions. Certainly it showed in a poor light the comparatively tawdry frocks and dresses of those around her. Yet there was something familiar about her.

Excusing himself, though by this time his present company were already three sheets to the wind, he crossed to her, with an assumed confidence partly buoyed by the beer bubbling inside.

He doffed his uniform cap. "Miss Hansen, isn't it?" Angus inquired politely. Kate feigned a moment of surprise, although she too had been surreptitiously inspecting the tall young man as resplendent as a peacock in the best dress uniform and rows and ribbons of medals.

"Yes...," she said, as if startled. "Angus Dunrow," Angus replied politely and gently shaking her hand. He took the bull by the horns: "I believe we once were neighbours. And I'm told you are now nursing with the delightful Sally Nkumu at the Hospital."

"You seem to know quite a bit about me," Kate glanced at Angus' epaulets..."Captain." Then she looked closely at him, this time from up close and almost reeled. "My God...you're that bloody terrorist from the Pool!"

"Guilty as charged, ma'am," Angus smiled widely with such obvious good humour that Kate couldn't help but notice the whiteness of his teeth against the deep, bush-imparted tan set against hair which could only be described as flaxen, with copper highlights. She was tall, but barely reached Angus' shoulder.

"Well you shouldn't creep up on people like that," Kate flared, trying to recover her composure, particularly when she remembered her exact state of undress at the time.

"Bugles and horns and warning shouts next time," Angus promised sincerely, the smile never wavering. Then seizing the moment while she was still unbalanced, he took her again by the hand and led her to the dance floor. By God, he's strong, Kate though rather irrelevantly. And impetuous. But she also found a certain satisfaction in knowing in her feminine soul that they would be the most outstanding couple on the floor, dancing to an orchestra which had now replaced Aunt Grace's wheezy organ. As long as he didn't dance like he sang, she suddenly feared.

That proved groundless. Angus glided across the floor with the grace and style of one to the manner born. And in turn, Angus found Kate almost weightless in his arms, anticipating each step and moving in total harmony with him. Kate, in turn, felt herself becoming increasingly melded with Angus and gave herself totally to the joy and dancing, something she hadn't experienced since well before leaving South Africa to come home.

The tune finally finished, but they stayed locked together for a long moment. "Wow," Kate managed, slightly breathlessly and not just from the exertion of the dance. "You certainly scrub up well, Captain."

"Your servant, ma'am," Angus smiled slightly mockingly, but with a twinkle in the green eyes. "But for the purposes of a pleasant afternoon, shall it be 'Angus....Kate?'"

Kate smiled back at him, a radiant smile. "Angus and Kate it is," she secretly liked the sound of the combination. "Now, in the name of compassion, would you buy a lady a drink?"

One Pimms became two, then three. Angus had switched to Scotch, though his eyes remained clear and his complexion bronzed. To his delight he found he and Kate shared a similar wicked sense of humour, of the absurd and also a distaste for hypocrisy and pomposity. Within an hour they were locked in an island of two, around which the hundred other guests eddied and flowed.

Their conversation flowed like the Zambezi in flood, with one immediately picking up where the other trailed off, sometimes in mid-sentence. Kate was quick-witted, with a keen eye for the ridiculous. She also obviously possessed a deep love for her profession and those in her care.

"We get quite a few of your chaps," she said at one stage and was unprepared for the sudden flash of anger on Angus' face and the way the warm green eyes became as flinty cold as icechips. But it was just for an instant and not directed at her but at the far horizon. A moment later he had relaxed and was once again smiling fully into her eyes. "Wow," Kate thought, "I've met a wild one here." Then she glanced at the rows of decorations across Angus' broad chest and wisely decided to leave the subject alone.

A moment later they were chatting like old friends, but each now delicately fencing with each other, probing for the unanswered questions which pave the way to a true relationship.

Angus, on the other hand, was becoming increasingly stricken with the enchanting young lady with him. He'd had more than his fair share of Bulawayo Bikes, the disparaging name for the young ladies of that town caught up in the heat of excitement and danger of the war, seeing their boyfriends go off to battle, sometimes never to return. But with Kate he sensed a basic purity of spirit – spirit which she had in abundance. And once he tore himself away from the bachelor instinct of wondering how beddable she might be, he found his respect growing for her ready wit and started to long for the beautiful smile which greeted some of his sallies.

"Angus old son," he wryly admitted to himself, "I think you might be smitten just a tad here." He began to prepare his campaign with as much care as if venturing into the bush in chase of a wounded lioness protecting her cubs. Because he had no doubt beneath the glowing soft exterior there would be claws. One did not grow up with Uncle Tom Hansen without being exposed to the realities of life.

Three Pimms became four. "God, the girl's got a hobnailed liver as well," he thought. Uncle Tom again. But then Kate looked a little mistily into his eyes.

"I think I'm becoming a tiny bit squiffed," she reluctantly admitted. The hot day, the excitement, the meeting finally with Angus Dunrow, whom she had secretly admired since her early teens, were taking their toll. "And dammit," she suddenly swore. "I have to drive back to Bulawayo now. I'm on duty tomorrow. And my old Volkswagen is spluttering like Uncle Tom on a bad morning." Angus grinned to himself...even his own daughter called the crusty old bugger Uncle Tom.

But he was nothing if not quick and charming. Besides a man would have to be deaf, blind and overwhelmingly stupid to let such a golden opportunity pass.

"By co-incidence, I have to be back in barracks tonight," he smoothly lied. "I'll drive you with pleasure and get Frikkie, our mechanic, to come over tomorrow and have a go at that bomb of yours."

Kate mock-fluttered her eyes at him. "Why sir, you are too kind," she murmured, laying a hand on Angus' arm. Her first gambit had succeeded! It was their first physical contact and Angus felt a tingle run up his arm and straight to where, if he didn't stand soon, he would only be able to do so with acute embarrassment.

They quickly did the rounds, thanking their hosts and farewelling those still standing. Some, particularly Angus' soldier friends, had brought bedrolls and intended making a real night of it all.

He led Kate around the house and ushered her into his British racing green Jaguar, judging by the sun they had about half an hour's daylight left. Plenty of time in the powerful car, which Angus drove swiftly and well, as though the half a dozen large scotches and several beers hadn't touched the sides.

He also drove with an almost total concentration, although the light hearted banter between them continued. It gave Kate an opportunity to openly study Angus in profile. That he was handsome was beyond question. In a masculine way with no softer lines, just a couple of whiter creases at the corners of his eyes from squinting in the African sun. But it was his green eyes which intrigued her. They were never still, flitting from road ahead to bush on either side and back to the road, lingering for no longer than a couple of seconds on each. Alert for possible ambush, she realised, although they were travelling a nearly one hundred miles an hour, hopefully fast enough to blast their way through an impromptu ambush. A well-set up one would be a totally different call.

As they hit the asphalt road on the final leg to Bulawayo, Angus relaxed slightly and shifted in his seat, but pushed the speed of the Jaguar even higher, so that it seemed just minutes before the lights of the outskirts of the city came into view.

Angus slowed and turned to smile to Kate. "Home sweet home," he said. Once again Kate was mesmerised by the warmth of that gesture. It seemed to come from deep within Angus and for some reason especially reserved for her alone.

Angus pulled up in front of the nurses' quarters and for a moment seemed to hesitate.

"Look," he began. He cleared his throat and started again. Kate was startled, but quietly amused...was the warrior just a little nervous about something? She found it a delicious thought.

"It's only early...the sun's just down," Angus continued. Kate concurred that the sun was, indeed, only just down. "I was wondering...hoping...that you might join me for dinner? I could pick you up in about an hour or so," he rushed on, suddenly committed to action. "That's if you would like to, of course," he blithered. Angus blushed within himself. He was carrying on like a love-forlorn teenager.

Kate, who had her fingers crossed for the past half an hour, pretended to consider. "I would love to," she said. "Of course, can't be too late...on duty tomorrow morning."

Angus, mopping imagined sweat from his brow, leapt from the driver's seat and hurried around to open the passenger's door, walking Kate to the front door. There was a moment of hesitation, then Kate, instinctively, raised herself onto her toes and pecked Angus on the cheek. "See you in an hour," she smiled into eyes.

Angus wasn't quite sure how he navigated to the family flat in town, but he found himself doing a quick step around the living room, with a Castle lager in hand. Joshua, the manservant who kept the place spick and span, looked on with amusement. Seldom in the past two years had he seen Angus in such a mood.

"A woman Nkosi?" he delicately inquired.

"Not just a woman, Josh," Angus declared loudly. "A jewel in the crown, a rose in the thorns, a sight so wondrous..." he trailed off.

"Perhaps Nkosi would like to shower while I lay out his evening dress?" Samson rose to the occasion.

Angus glanced at his watch. "My God! Quickly man, I have half an hour to be there."

Resplendent, but smartly casually dressed in immaculately ironed cream slacks, a navy blue blazer and the regimental tie, Angus roared up to the steps of the nursing quarters with perhaps a minute to spare. Quickly checking his hair in the mirror, he entered through the portal of the nurses quarters – in the not so distant past that it had in itself had been a major task akin to St George tackling the Dragon in its den, such was the motherly ferousity of the matron in charge of the quarters.

But times had mellowed, tragically mainly due to the steady stream of young wounded soldiers coming into the hospital and the often inhumane hours the nurses were forced to work. The matron had mellowed and now she greeted Angus with a smile and a nod to the waiting room.

Angus entered and there Kate was, simply although beautifully dressed in an evening dress in black which accentuated both her figure and the startling blue eyes. "My God, you're beautiful," Angus blurted as he offered his arm. Kate not only took the proffered arm but seemed to snuggle just a tad closer than strictly necessary.

"I'll say it again...Angus," she murmured. "You scrub up well."

Angus drove to the Bulawayo Club, where he had taken the precaution of booking a discreet and private booth in the dining room. Immaculately starched waiters hovered and they both settled on a dry martini before settling on studying the menu, which was as comprehensive as anything on offer from Cape Town north.

Eventually, they both settled for fish, complemented with succulent prawns and delicious crayfish tails, washed down with an excellent Sauvignon Blanc from a little-known but excellent vineyard from the Paarl.

Angus was pleased to see that Kate's appetite was almost as robust as his own and despite the earlier flood of Pimms she showed no effect from the alcohol. In fact, he silently pondered, they were drunk on each others' company.

Afterwards, Angus wondered where the night had gone. It seemed one moment they had been ushered to the table, the next they were sipping a fine cognac with their coffee. There had been no awkward pauses, nothing to break the spell of their ... and Angus surruptiously checked his watch ... 12 hour relationship because it was going to be a relationship. Of that Angus had never been more deadly serious.

Kate, for her part had seldom taken her eyes from Angus. The secret, she decided, was his absolute sincerity. When he looked into her eyes he seemed to be looking into her soul. And he was delightful company. Attentive, funny, serious when the time called for it. No, my girl, she thought, this one is not going to get away. But then she remembered his career and a sudden chill seemed to run down her spine so that suddenly the coffee and cognac tasted sour.

Angus noted immediately the subtle change and misinterpreted. "My God, it's late and I promised you an early night," he exclaimed, moving around the table to assist her from the booth. "Better get you back before the Dragon thinks I have kidnapped you for immoral purposes!"

"If only," Kate kept the thought well within her. Angus drove sedately back to the quarters, both of them wrapped in a comfortable silence. A hundred metres before the entrance there was a small grove of trees and Angus coasted to a stop.

"Car trouble...probably petrol," he began, but Kate was already reaching for him. The first kiss was the release of pent up emotion and she felt almost helpless as his powerful arms locked around her. But hers had involuntarily locked around his neck as she devoured the kiss, making tiny mewing noises. If a kiss could last forever, it seemed this one did, but they both eventually broke for breath.

"Wow!" Kate murmured. "And how," Angus smiled as he agreed. They came together again, this time with gentleness, their fingertips exploring each others' faces. Kate eventually snuggled her head into Angus' shoulder and softly ran her fingers though his soft and thick hair.

They lay entwined for a few more minutes, then Kate eventually stirred. "The Dragon may have mellowed, but not all that much," she smiled. Angus grinned, and shifting upright started the Jag. "Ah...petrol problem appears to have cleared," he said, deadpan. They drove in silence to the entry.

"Angus," Kate hated to break the mood. "How long do we have before you have to...and her voice grow smaller and tailed off. Angus understood immediately. "All week," he said. "I'm on leave until then." If Kate noticed the discrepancy between Angus' initial excuse to drive her back to Bulawayo and this version, she wisely gave no clue.

"I'm on early shift all this week," she said, the practical side of the nurse emerging. "But where can we meet? This is a nice car, but that damn gearstick is a bloody nuisance."

Angus laughed outright. "My family keeps a flat in town. It's where I stay when I'm not at the barracks."

"Perfect," Kate purred. She leaned over and kissed him once more. "Don't get out...the Dragon will get suspicious." Angus grinned at her..."How are you going to stop her getting suspicious if you are spending every night in the company of such as well-known rascal as me," he teased.

"Angus Dunrow," Kate flared. "I am over 21 and perfectly entitled to spend my free time any way I choose. Plus I have a sick aunt who I must see to from time to time."

"Do you?" Angus asked, suddenly concerned. "Of course not, you damned terrorist/warrior," Kate said. With that she kissed Angus one last time with such passion it almost drove his head into the side window, patted him on the knee and leaving the car walked into the quarters.

Angus sat still for a full five minutes. He tried in vain to think of a time when he had felt more alive, but gave up. He considered his options. He was far too ebullient to go home and eventually decided a few brandies with those remaining in the public bar at the Club would be the perfect end to a perfect evening. Might even take a game of snooker or two off that pompous git Richard Amery.

He knew that, barring emergencies, Kate was through for the day by about 3pm, so at 3.15 Angus pulled up outside the quarters. Instead of the gleaming Jaguar, he drove his bush car, a highly modified Land Rover which despite the scratches and bashes on the panels had been painstakingly rebuilt by Frikkie. He was also dressed in bush clothes, casual khakis with a loose-fitting shirt he left untucked. On his feet were a pair of well-worn, but cared-for veldshoens. He had warned Kate it was casual dress and she had responded appropriately.

She blanched, however, when she saw the mode of transport waiting for her, particularly when Angus had to vault into the open-top Rover and kick open the passenger door from inside.

"Where on earth do you think you are taking me in this, Angus Dunrow," she archly inquired.

"All good things come to those with patience," Angus leered suggestively at her and booted the huge engine into life. On the outskirts of Bulawayo he swung into what could be charitably be called a track, rough, stone-ridden and crowded with thorn bushes. He still drove fast; to overcome the ruts in the track, but Kate could sense the difference. Angus appeared almost carefree, swapping jokes, including a few of the ribald ones. Kate leant back and decided she liked this version of Angus just as much, perhaps even more than the previous night's model.

After half an hour of bush-bashing, with Angus wrestling the wheel and occasionally swearing under his breath, they breached the top of a difficult hill and Angus halted the wagon. He wanted Kate to savour the moment. Before them lay a rarity in Matabeleland, a beautiful small lake with natural grasses shaded by a grotto of acacia trees.

"Ours," he said to Kate. "Just ours for now." They gently motored down the steep decline and came to a halt near the natural picnic ground. Angus had come well-prepared, with picnic baskets full of delicacies and another containing ice – and champagne. And a picnic rug which would have done justice to a king-sized bed.

It was one of those glorious days in Matabeland, cloudless and warm, just warm enough to raise a trickle of sweat on them both. Kate lay back on the rug and stretched like a contented cat.

"This is beautiful Angus," she murmured. Of all the places so far removed from the urgency of the emergency ward, Angus had chosen with unerring accuracy and perception, she realised.

Angus popped the first bottle of champagne and poured into two Waterford crystal flutes, giving one to Kate with a smile and a flourish. "Madam would care for refreshment?"

Kate laughed. "Angus, you are priceless," she managed and then quickly revised the words in her mind. No, she firmly decided, he *was* priceless. Of course she knew of Angus' reputation among the Bulawayo female population, but when she looked at him, she saw no guile, just the same open-to-the-soul green eyes.

A second glass of champagne, Moet Chandon, she noted irrelevantly was poured and Kate visibly relaxed. Angus casually lit a cigarette. Funny, but she hadn't noticed him smoking previously. However, in tobacco-rich Rhodesia it was almost unpatriotic not to smoke.

A friendly and comfortable silence grew between them. "It's growing sticky," Angus finally broke the silence. "A swim?" Now the smile was almost a devil's leer, Kate decided, then looked again. No, it *was* a devil-may-care smile.

"I...I didn't bring any togs," Kate stammered in a slight confusion. Angus' only reaction was a slight crease between his eyebrows and a broad smile. "A little too late for that minor detail, wouldn't you have thought?" he said. "Although I've made sure the shotgun is safely in the wagon."

Bugger you, Mr Angus Dunrow, Kate thought, as the blush from the memory of that day by the Pool came rushing back. "Last one in is a sissy," she shouted over her shoulder as she shed her clothes in lightning speed and sprinted towards the water. Angus was slightly hamstrung by the glass of champagne she had handed back to him in her haste to disrobe, but quickly dragged his own clothes off. Besides, he was enjoying the sight of bouncing boobs and backside designed for far more important things than riding a horse.

Kate dived in first, gasping at first with the cold, then quickly pivoted to watch Angus sprint to the water's edge. My God in heaven, she thought. Adonis eat your heart out. Angus was not heavily built, nor overly hairy. But he possessed the body of an athlete trained to Olympic perfection, each muscle rippling in perfect co-ordination with the others, broad shoulders, strong chest, tapering to slim but powerful hips. His legs, the legacy of countless hundreds of miles of patrolling in the bush – and tough farm work were in themselves a work of art. Quickly she glanced to his private parts and almost moaned. Perfect in every regard, she admitted.

She lost him for a moment in the sun as he dived in, only to be suddenly seized by her ankles and dragged under the water. Spluttering she came up to air, to find herself face to face, and breast to chest, with Angus.

Instinctively her arms went around his neck as his went around her waist, Angus could stand in the pool, which put her at a slight disadvantage, but she pushed her body against his as they kissed. Angus began caressing her body, working his hands from her shoulders to her rounded buttocks and back. Kate began to feel the most delicious of heat rising within her and with a very feminine satisfaction felt Angus' almost immediate response.

She was rapidly becoming in urgent need of this man, a dispassionate part of her mind registered, a thought which flew when Angus cupped her buttocks once again and guided her legs around him. "For God's sake stop teasing me," she groaned and groaned again with satisfaction and pleasure as he entered her. She leant slight backwards to allow him full access and also to free her breasts for his increasingly urgent caresses.

Nothing else for either existed. The world had gone away, replaced by their increasingly urgent love making. Both were young, vibrant and totally swept away with the absolute joy of being as close as was possible. Both, too, had gone far too long without love and it was with increasingly urgency Angus powered his way towards climax...and as he groaned and strained Kate reached towards her own climax, partially smothering her screams of delight and fulfilment by biting on Angus's shoulder. It spurred Angus to greater heights and, as one, they reached their peak together.

For long minutes they remained entwined, then slowly disengaged and Kate floated on her back, her head on Angus' shoulder and she gently nuzzled his neck and kissed his cheek. Angus slowly opened his eyes and gently smiled down at her. She was struck by the new definition of depth in those green depths. There was no need for words.

"Angus my darling," Kate eventually murmured, breaking the silence.

"Angus my darling," she dreamily repeated.

Eventually Angus shook his curls like a water-logged spaniel. He grinned. "We have champagne growing warm and an afternoon tea to die for," he said. "Man does not live by love alone, wench."

"You can be such a romantic bastard sometime Angus Dunrow," Kate retorted, though her heart had backflipped. Angus had mentioned love? Now that, she determined, was a diamond worth far more exploration.

Still naked, they lay on the picnic rug while Angus opened another Moet Chandon and laid out a feast from the baskets. Angus, for his part, was happy to devour the sight of the naked Kate, reaching to her to gently caress another secret part, gently tickling her belly when she least expected it so that Kate almost choked on caviar. Kate on the other hand was equally studying Angus, watching the gently rise and fall of his chest as he ripped chicken apart and cut the cheeses.

Eventually, both sated they enjoyed the last of the afternoon's sunshine. Then, in accord as one they reached for each other. This time the lovemaking was slow and tender, each building the other up, relaxing for a sip of champagne and resuming where they left off. And this time there were no sudden explosions, their eyes almost touching as they gazed with utmost tenderness into each others' souls as they reached the finale.

It was now almost completely dark and Angus packed the picnic gear into the Land Rover. Kate looked around, slightly concerned. "What about terrs," she asked. Angus smiled. "Not on this track," he said. "If they are about they will be moving into positions around farms. Besides," and he pointed to the fully-stocked gun rack attached to the rollbar just behind the seats. "We could liven them on their way a little."

And sure enough, although the track remained as arduous as before, they struck no trouble, the powerful spotlights reaching out a mile ahead. Back on the asphalt, Angus let the powerful Rover have its head, maintaining a speed just short of that achieved by the Jaguar. They rolled into Bulawayo and instead of turning into the road for the nurses' quarters, which Kate had secretly feared, Angus kept driving to one of the city's more upmarket areas.

What he had rather disparagingly described as a "flat" to Kate turned out to be something far more luxurious, a purpose-built large apartment, with four bedrooms, a huge living area and a kitchen which would not have disgraced a restaurant. It had highly polished yellow wood floor boards with rich and thick rugs scattered liberally throughout and walls decked with paintings which even Kate, which her untrained eye, could tell were masterpieces of the African landscape and animal life.

Yet something was missing. "You have no trophies on the walls, no skins on the floors?" she asked Angus. "My family does not, and never has, hunted animals for trophies," he replied. "It is their land as much as ours."

Suddenly that simple statement brought home a whole new meaning of the world of Angus Dunrow to Kate. It went a long way to explain his anti-racist beliefs, his deep friendship with Daniel and Sally, the Dunrow family's willingness to sub-let part of their farm to their black neighbours. "It is their land as much as ours." Such a simple statement, such a deep meaning.

The week Angus had promised Kate flew past. He would be waiting outside the quarters just after 3pm, just enough time for her to quickly shower and change. Then they let the day dictate their movements, swinging from a mood for an afternoon swim in the lake to a leisurely drive into the surrounding veldt, stealthily stalking up on giraffe, kudu, impala and zebra. Once, to both of their delight, they across a massive old bull elephant strolling across the land where once he had roamed for thousands of miles at will. Kate discovered where the photos in the apartment originated, because Angus carried an expensive Canon camera with a large zoom lens. Not once did he touch the guns in the rack.

Once he took her to the golf club for an impromptu lesson, where Kate distinguished herself by falling flat on her behind with her first mad attack on the little ball. But with Angus nestled in behind her and slowing the momentum down she finally hit a few decent shots down the fairway. "Okay, big shot," Kate said. "Do better than that."

Angus smiled and taking a driver and teeing the ball, he effortlessly drove it nearly out of sight. "It's all in the mind," he said, as Kate gasped. "Think positive. I just thought of you as I hit the ball...beautifully formed and perfectly in balance."

Kate looked at him with mock severity, "Angus Dunrow, you have one of the finest developed talents for bullshit I have ever encountered." And with that she kissed him fully on the mouth, to the cheers and applause from members sitting on the club veranda.

As evening closed in they would eat in fabulous little restaurants where Angus always seemed on first name terms with the owner and then drift in one mind back to the apartment.

Their love making was always divine, lifting each other to new heights, in the giant king-sized bed in Angus' room. Joshua had always prepared a late supper and discreetly repaired to his quarters. Kate had by this time moved spare uniforms into the apartment. "I am, after all, over 21," she explained to Angus. So each morning, after the obligatory warming up, welcome-to-the-new-day loving he would drop her to the hospital.

But then suddenly it was Friday afternoon and Kate finally mustered the courage to ask the question which had been at the forefront of her mind most of the week. "Angus darling," she murmured as she lay snuggled into his arms. "You're back on duty tomorrow."

Angus rolled over and regarded her through eyes made languid with love making. "Not until Sunday night," he said. "And I know you are off duty this weekend, so I had a special plan in mind."

He kept her in suspense until she mock hit him on the chest. "What is it, you devious bastard?" she asked.

"Well...I thought a picnic by the Pool at Hillview," he said. "Ride the horses," he paused as a sudden thought struck him. "Where do you keep that beautiful filly?"

"God Angus, you can be so blind sometimes," Kate replied. "In the Hillview stables of course."

Angus grinned. "Of course." He continued "Then we can stay the night at the farm. I've already warned Matilda that a special dinner for two will be required,"

"And what," Kate asked archly. "If I had other plans? One of my many other beaux?" Angus nodded seriously. "Then I would have to maim them, one by one so as I was your only choice left."

In response Kate rolled fully on top of Angus and proceeded to teach him how unnecessary other beaux were...as if there had been any to begin with she smugly grinned.

They left almost at first light, giving the early morning patrol trucks time to run down the road first against the chance of an overnight mine being planted. The terrs had been known to tunnel under the asphalt, plant the explosive and wait for the unfortunate first truck in the convoy before opening fire with their Ak47's on the remaining trucks.

Angus paused the Jag at the first roadblock heading out of Bulawayo, casually nodding at the sentries. "Any bad news ahead," he inquired. "All quiet?" The black sentry saluted, although Angus was not in uniform in military circles he was somewhat of a legend. "All quiet, Sah," he confirmed. Angus thanked him courteously and planted his foot on the accelerator. Typical, Kate thought, the man only has one speed, flat out. But then she remembered his gently stroking and quiet hugging and blushed.

"What devilment do you have in mind?" Angus queried. "You only blush like that about one thing."

"Shut up, Dunrow," Kate snapped, but could help the blush which continued to rise on her face. Angus laughed, the laugh of a man with no care in the world, a beautiful woman by his side, a powerful car at his fingertips and the prospect of a day at his much-loved home. If this is love, he pondered, I'm all in favour. So far he hadn't been able to bring those fateful words to his lips, but very soon he knew. Which started a related school of thought. Why hadn't he? He knew in his heart they were the words Kate wanted to hear more than anything, the final cement to hold the rock solid foundation they were building together.

Okay, it had been just a week. But that week had stretched an eternity. She was everything he wanted in a woman and, more importantly, a partner. She loved the land as he did, she shared his passions as he shared hers. She was beautiful, she laughed with the ease of one who enjoyed all life had to offer. But then, he reflected, there was the bloody War, hanging over the whole Rhodesian society. Would life ever been normal again? He secretly hoped so, but more realistically doubted it.

Those thoughts lasted all the way to the turnoff to the dusty road to the farm. Kate, watching Angus though the corner of her eye, realised he was deep in reflection and remained silent.

But at the turnoff at Mbelo, it was as if a light had suddenly been switched on. Angus turned in his seat and grinned at Kate. "Katey, my darling, welcome back to God's own land," he said. The dust billowed behind the Jag as they powered the remaining 20 minutes to Hillview, Angus only slowing to pull in through the gates.

Angus eased himself from the car and leisurely stretched, then walking around to open Kate's door. "Angus," Kate urgently whispered. "I am not getting out and for God's sake get back in and lock the door." Angus looked at her in perplexity. "Why?"

"Because," and Kate pointed with a trembling finger, "There is a bloody great lion on your stoep. Angus followed the direction of her aimed finger and let out a bellow of delight.

"Tom!" he shouted ecstatically. "Tommy boy!" The massive lion, a veteran of many seasons, lazily looked up and suddenly locked his yellow eyes on Angus. If Angus' bellow was loud, Tom's roar seemed to shake Hillview's foundations. He sprang to his paws and charged Angus. Stretched to his full height, he planted a hugely muscular leg around each of Angus' shoulders and almost seeming to purr as he rubbed his massive mane into Angus' head.

Angus hugged Tom with all his strength and then pushed him away. "Get off me, you stupid bastard," he said as Tom rolled on his back like a gigantic pussy cat and then contented himself with rubbing his length along Angus' calf, where he easily reached his waist, all the time rumbling with delight.

"You can come out now," Angus turned to the car and a wide-eyed Kate. "Tom meet Kate, Kate meet Tom," he introduced them. Tom reluctantly detached himself from Angus and padded over to Kate, where he sniffed her and then looked at Angus with what he interpreted as a nod of approval.

"He knows you now," Angus explained. Kate looked at Angus with a look he couldn't fathom. "Can we please go inside the house and have a stiff drink and you can tell me about this tall tale?" she asked.

"I found Tom as an abandoned cub out near the Pool," he explained. His mother had rejected the cub and Tom was as skinny as a kitten. Angus had coaxed the little fellow with infinite patience to first come near him and then gently stroked the baby lion. Tom had slowly responded, first arching his back, then cocking his head as Angus tickled him behind his ear. Angus had finally put the cub into his carry-all small kit bag and ridden slowly home, so as not to disturb Tom. He'd walked into the kitchen door as Matilda was overseeing the evening's meal and with his finger to his mouth to indicate silence had nodded at the bag. Matilda was used to Angus bringing home all sorts of lost and lame animals, but something in his eyes moved her to caution. She peaked inside the bag, to be met with a beautiful pair of yellow eyes staring back at her.

"Angie," she shook her head in mock disapproval. "This time you have really overdone it. A lion? What in the name of the Gods are you going to do with *this*?"

"Keep him, of course, until he's old enough to fend for himself," Angus explained. "But, 'Tilde, this is our secret." Matilda had rustled through the storage room until she found an old baby's bottle with a small teat and filled it with lukewarm milk and a couple of tiny vitamin supplements. She gently lifted Tom from the bag and, as if with a weaning baby gave him a sniff of the mixture. It took Tom all of 10 seconds to get the message and he guzzled the food, until his tiny tummy was bloated. They found a small basket and a warm but secure place on the outdoor veranda.

Angus had looked at the tiny creature and finally shook his head. "This won't do at all," he said. He picked up Tom, basket and all and carried him to his own bedroom. Tom didn't seem at all perturbed by the sudden change from living in the rough to the comfortable and warm room and was almost immediately asleep.

Angus tiptoed, quite unnecessarily from the room, joining Matilda for a cup of tea. "I dearly want to watch you explain this one to your parents," she admonished Angus, who smiled warmly to her. "Just another stray, you old busybody," he teased her. "He'll be out and about in no time."

He spent the rest of the afternoon doing a few chores around the house, but his mind was firmly fixed on Tom. "Why Tom?" Matilda had queried. "He reminds me of Uncle Tom," he said and even as a devout Christian, who attended the farm church regularly, Matilda had crossed her fingers against any possible hex.

Angus could not resist the temptation any longer and softly went to his room. Instead of a peaceful cub sleeping in a basket, there was no longer a basket to be seen. It was shredded across the bedroom where Tom had obviously woken and decided it was playtime. Instead, he was now firmly ensconced on Angus' bed, snoring softly on what remained of the chewed up feather pillows and obviously quite satisfied with his afternoon's work.

And so Tom became part of the Dunrow clan, but not without strenuous objections from his parents. "A bloody lion!" Jonathon had thundered on a rare visit to the farm. "Sleeping on your bed? God almighty man, what the *hell* are you going to bring home next? A fucking hippo?" Since Jonathon rarely swore it was a measure of his discontent. Angus' mother had simply looked him in the eyes are gave a long-suffering sigh. They already had an orphans' zoo on the side of the stables.

Tom showed no signs of discomfort whatsoever. On a steady diet he grew at an alarming rate. Which was to be expected, Angus thought. Tom had feet almost the size of dinner plates. He had taken to basking in the sun in the small courtyard enclosure outside of Angus' room, showing every sign that if not king of the jungle, he was master of the courtyard.

But one day Angus came home from an arduous day on the farm and Tom was nowhere to be seen either in the bedroom or in the courtyard. Angus resigned himself to the fact that Tom had heard the call of the wild, until he raised his vision to the top of the seven foot wall enclosing his private garden and saw Tom majestically lying there, legs either side of the foot-wide wall and gazing off into the distance in between lion-napping.

As Tom grew he became more attached to Angus, following him like a faithful dog around the house, into the yard and even paced up and down the swimming pool as Angus did his daily 100 laps. His diet changed as well and the day came when reluctantly Angus took one of the smaller calibre sports rifles and drove out to where he knew a herd of kudo gathered. Selecting an old bull, past his breeding prime, Angus killed him cleanly with one shot. He needed the winch to haul the beast into the back of the farm wagon and drove back to the makeshift abattoir well away from the house. He efficiently gutted the bull and hacked off a haunch, leaving the rough skin attached.

Tom took to the haunch like a delightful new toy, mock-growling at it, throwing in the air and catching it in his mouth. On the third attempt, his teeth pierced the skin and all games came to an abrupt end. He devoured the entire haunch over two days leaving it only reluctantly when Angus appeared. The entire beast lasted just a fortnight. And Tom grew towards being the magnificent lion he would become, his coat glossy and his mane beginning to grow into an emperor's crown around his noble head.

However, Angus knew that if Tom was to survive in the wild, not that he gave any indication of abandoning the Dunrow Palace for Orphaned Lions, he would need to develop hunter skills.

Angus started by sedately riding Nelson to more isolated regions of the farm, where wildlife was almost guaranteed, Tom loping along in their wake. They came across a herd of gemsbok and although Tom showed intense concentration it was clear he did not associate them with food. In their natural state, lions are among nature's laziest creatures, content to lie in the shade of bushes while the lionesses do the work of rounding up the targets and killing sufficient to feed the pride. The lion though, of course, has first rights at the dinner table.

"Well," Angus told Tom, "I can't rustle you up a missus so you are going to have do some work. Do you good, get some of the fat off you." Time and again Angus had caught himself talking to Tom as one would a smart dog. That night, there was no kudu to feast on at the homestead and Tom looked at Angus with hurt eyes.

The next day, and the next, they rode out again. On the third day, however, something seemed to click in Tom's mind and instead of curiously studying the gemsbok he lowered onto his haunches and became stalking through the bush. Angus dismounted and loosely threw Nelson's reigns around a convenient branch. He, in turn, stalked Tom, absorbed by the animal's almost complete concentration on the task in hand.

Tom would remain absolutely motionless for minutes, then creep forward, carefully disguised in the bush. Angus was pleased to see the big cat had instinctively remained downwind of the herd. Finally, Tom was just metres away and it apparent he had chosen his prey. A succulent female, well-covered with fat from the rich grazing land.

He exploded from the bush with an amazing blast of speed and before the gemsbok was aware, he had her in the death tackle, powerful jaws clamped around the neck and rolling his target on the ground, instantly breaking her neck. Tom sniffed her for a moment then raised his head and roared like Angus had never heard from him before. It was the roar of a warrior, a champion who had conquered.

The remaining gemsbok herd had scattered to the winds, deathly afraid of one of their most feared predators. Tom buried his head into the still warm blood flowing from the gemsbok and seemed to temporarily drink and eat his fill.

Angus had crept away. He wanted Tom to savour the moment, the instant he had bonded with the bush which was his natural home. But part of him felt a sadness. He knew that now Tom had begun to learn the ways of the wild his time at the Dunrow homestead would become increasingly rare.

It was almost as if Tom had read his thoughts, because he effortlessly picked up his prey and proudly made his way back to Angus and Nelson, blood dripping from his fangs. If lions could smile, Angus thought, Tom would be on the stage. He carried himself more erect, his carriage more regal. He looked at Angus as if to say "what are we waiting for?" and began to march back to the farmhouse. It was only a mile or so and Tom led the way, pausing now and then to shake the dead gemsbok in his jaws as if to reassure himself it had actually happened.

Angus never again went shooting for Tom. Occasionally he would wake, to find the huge lion missing, having leapt the wall during the night to stalk further food. He never came back empty jawed, though his diet became more varied.

But there were to odd incidents which didn't add to Tom's appeal his appeal to Angus' mother, Elizabeth. One afternoon she was hosting a bridge party in the formal parlour with three very proper ladies from nearby farms.

Suddenly one of the matrons screamed and threw her cards in the air. So intent had she been on winning the rubber on an audacious two no-trump opening bid she hadn't noticed Tom enter the room. He was curious and leant his giant head on the erstwhile lady's lap, gazing solemnly into her eyes. Feeling the weight, the no-trumpery had looked down at the most ferious creature she had ever seen. She promptly fainted. Elizabeth shouted at Angus in most unladylike language "Tom get out. Angus," even louder, "Come and get this bloody lion out of here. That's it, he is bloody banned from the house." It took smelling salts and three stiff brandies before the bridge player could string two words together.

Angus, to make matters worse, had laughed. But from then, Tom was confined to quarters – Angus' quarters – and only allowed on the stoep, a situation he accepted with equaniminity.

When Angus was away on war duties, Tom simply disappeared. For weeks he wouldn't be sighted. But uncannily, within an hour or so of Angus coming home Tom would be back, welcoming Augus with play fights and rasping his tongue over Angus' often filthy uniforms, which were usually only good enough for the incinerator.

* * *

"See Kate," Angus now explained. "Tom knew I was coming."

Kate tossed her second gin and tonic, easy on the tonic, and looked at Angus. "You really are a remarkable man, Angus Dunrow," she quietly said. Angus chuckled. "Life is for living, my sweet."

They changed into riding clothes and went down to the stables, where the grooms had saddled and prepared Sunshine, Kate's filly whose full pedigree name, Golden Rainbow Mistress, had been promptly dropped. Angus let out his two-toned whistle and once again Nelson came thundering across the paddock, sniffing expectantly for a mango while Angus prepared him. Once again he holstered two guns and once again Matilda had prepared a picnic fit for royalty. Tom comfortably paced along behind them.

Nelson sniffed Sunshine for a moment and returned his attention to Angus. Companionly, they rode close, almost touching at a sedate pace out to the Pool. On the natural grass Angus unsaddled the horses and let them graze while he prepared the picnic lunch. "Swim first?" he asked Kate. "Fuck *swim* first, Dunrow," Kate replied with the determined look in her eye he had come to recognise as she undressed as quickly as possible. "Swim later," Angus amicably agreed and he followed suit, taking her in his arms so they fell together onto the rug with an overwhelming urgency.

Kate eventually rolled to her favourite position, chin on Angus' shoulder with her solemn eyes looking though his to the depth of his soul. She finally allowed herself to think the deeply repressed thought. "Angus Dunrow, I love you and if you get yourself killed in this bloody war I will never forgive you," she silently said to herself. But it was as if Angus had read her mind.

He lent to her lips and very gently kissed her, caressing the back of her slender neck.

"Swim now?" he mocked with that easy half smile she had grown to treasure. It seemed reserved for her only. "Swim now," she agreed and they slowly rose and arm in arm walked slowly into the beautiful clear water. Finally it was only the cold which drove them out of the Pool, to bask in the sun. A sudden thought struck Kate. "Would Tom have been here that...that first time we met?" she asked.

Angus laughed. "Almost certainly. But he's too well fed to be bothered with a skinny little creature like you."

The silence and peace was suddenly shattered by a violent splash in the Pool. The temptation had finally grown too much for Nelson and from a running start he launched himself right out in mid-Pool.

Snuffling with pleasure he showed the true meaning behind horseplay. Sunshine intently looked at him and delicately placed a forelock in the shallows. With a lady-like shiver she retired to the comfort of the sunshine, joining Tom who was lying on his back, legs akimbo and snoring.

"Typical woman," Angus observed and was rewarded with a smack on his behind by Kate. One thing inevitably led to the inevitable and the sun was beginning to wane into the sudden African dusk when they eventually saddled the horses and headed back for the farmhouse.

The night would be chilly and the servants had prepared a roaring log fire in the enormous fireplace in the main living room, a room with large comfortable chairs and couches and rugs scattered over the floor.

The both changed into more suitable casual evening clothing and Angus dragged a couch over to near the fire so they could warm their feet as they sipped a sundowner. Angus had a Jamesons Irish whiskey, for which he had developed a taste while visiting that beautiful green country and Kate ordered a dry martini.

Matilda had thoughtfully had the servants set up an intimate table for two in the room and judging from the delicious aroma occasionally wafting through it was to be a special meal indeed. Angus uncorked one the special bottles of shiraz he had been saving and when they were ready to eat, picked up a small silver bell and rang it twice. Gideon, who could have snapped up a job in any of Bulawayo's top restaurants, immediately appeared with entree, an oxtail soup such as Kate had never tasted.

"It's in the herbs," Angus explained. "All grown here."

Course followed course, a second bottle of shiraz washing down the feast. Finally Kate admitted defeat. Angus, who was also feeling more than replete, rose and drew back the chair for Kate. They resumed their positions on the fireside couch, nestling comfortably in each others' arms and nursing a brandy.

"Kate, my love, whatever am I do with you," he eventually murmured into Kate's blonde hair. Kate made no response save for tightening her hold around Angus. He gently kissed to top of her head and they both relaxed into the silence only special occasions warrant.

Once Angus had shoo-ed Tom off the bed they lay closely entwined and deep sleep came to both of them almost simultaneously.

Despite the huge preceding day, and the amount of booze they had consumed, both were awake early and again it was the most natural start to the day to possess each other, starting snoozily and building to a climax which had the king-sized bed rocking.

And as they emerged for breakfast on the stoep Matilda couldn't help but give Angus a sly wink when she was sure Kate wasn't watching. That she heartedly approved of Kate was underlined by the delicate cuts of bacon and wonderfully poached eggs, which came with tropical fruit and a deep, flavoursome coffee. Angus in turn was handed a couple of rough cuts of ham and scrambled eggs. He poured his own coffee.

Kate lent back in the morning sun and stretched luxuriously. "What a beautiful day," she sighed with contentment. "How long to we have?" The rest of our life if I had my way, Angus thought but replied: "We must leave after lunch. So it's your choice, my darling. Tennis? A horse ride? Swim?" he indicated the pool.

Kate shook her head. "I'd like to sit here in the sun and savour the morning quietly, perhaps find a book to read." She looked anxious for a moment. "Do you mind?"

Angus chuckled. "I'd like to be in some form of awakedness when I report. A casual morning it is." He rose and went into the HillView library, coming back with a selection of books ranging from handpainted illustrations of the wilderness and its inhabitants to a couple of thrillers.

Kate tucked her legs underneath her in that uniquely feminine pose and became immediately absorbed in the wilderness album, so deeply engrossed that a tiny frown of concentration formed a V between her eyes.

Angus went inside and changed into swimming togs and without haste leisurely swam 100 laps, with Tom faithfully keeping pace. All the bugger needs is a stop watch and he'd make a first-rate trainer, Angus thought, not for the first time.

He called for fruit juice for them both and lay back on the settee, soaking in the sun with a sensual pleasure. Eyes closed, he drifted into a gentle slumber and so was unaware that Kate had abandoned her book and was closely studying him. Not his physical presence, of which she knew plenty, but the look on Angus face as he slept. The lines had smoothed, the hair was tousled and his eyelashes caught the golden rays of the sun.

In so many ways a youth, untouched by the world, she thought, then felt a jolt of fear as she remembered his reputation as a soldier. One of the most highly decorated in Rhodesia, leader of the elite Leopard group, the best among the best. She shuddered and reached over to brush his hair from his forehead. "Stay safe," my warrior, my love," she silently prayed.

It seemed just minutes before Gideon appeared with the gin and tonic aperitifs. Lunch was a casual affair, a light curry on saffron rice with pappadums, washed down with icy beer. Eventually Angus rose and stretched. "Witching hour," I'm afraid," he said. "Time to make tracks." A thought occurred to him "By the way, Frikkie fixed your Volkswagon, but became so enthralled with what he could do for it, he's taken it apart again and says he's going to make it the fastest in the country."

Kate blanched. "I really don't want the fastest Beetle in Rhodesia," she said. "And...how am I to get around?"

Angus looked taken aback, then smiled. "In the Jag, of course. I certainly won't be using it. Plus," and he smiled. "You'll find it easier to transport your gear to the apartment. Kate was once again flummoxed. "Your apartment," she echoed. "Yep," Angus replied. Unless you are particularly partial to that rathole they call the nurses' quarters."

"But..." Kate stammered..."Your parents?" Angus looked at her in amusement. "They have both fallen in love with you and have been giving me a hard time for not finding you before." He kicked the ground absently with his boot and looked steadily at Kate. "Which I suppose gives me the opening I'm been searching for."

Kate looked at him intently. "Why Angus," she teased. "You're blushing." She paused for a moment to tease him further. "What opening?" she archly inquired.

Angus drew closer to her and gazed down into her eyes. "Kate Hansen," he began, then coughed and started again. "Katey, I love you."

Tears sprang to Kate's eyes and she rushed into his arms. "Christ, what have I done now," Angus blurted, alarmed as all men are by sudden tears.

"You great big idiot," Kate said between snuffles. "I couldn't live without you. I love you more than I could even begin to say."

"Remember also there is a guest wing at the apartment," Angus argued practically and received and painful kick in the shin for his effort. "Just say you love me again, please," she pleaded.

"Katey, I love you more than life itself," Angus quietly said. "Without you, I am nowhere."

Chapter Six

"This is the big one chaps," the Colonel addressed the meeting hall, which for once had its full continent of Leopards. Those who had been in the bush on clandestine assignments had been urgently recalled. All leave was cancelled. No-one was to leave the base.

"We're going after the bastards, into Mozambique." Here, he pointed to a large-scale map on the podium. "About 100 clicks in, to be precise. A chance aerial photo has shown us a massive training camp. The boffins have analysed it until they can analyse no more. There are trenches, command bunkers, gunnery ranges and they estimate at least five thousand terrs in training."

Here, he paused, to wipe his foggy glasses, then continued: "The aim is simple, the orders come from the top, to wipe them out." He looked to Angus, on the stage with him. "Your turn."

Angus deliberately paused, looking at the individual members of the unit.

"This," he began, "is a Scouts operation, they've planned it, they've disguised ten trucks as Mozambique FRELIMO vehicles and they are going in black-faced. They want to convince the terrs they have come to help and train. They believe the terrs will flood towards the trucks – particularly when they shout out 'Zimabwe is ours, the war has finished'. The first four will carry only Black troopers so initially that ruse should work. Then, when all the trucks are in position they will open fire with everything they have. It should be like scything corn in the field.

"Our job is secondary – but vital. The Scouts are taking on about 5000 terrs in a full-frontal attack; it's inevitable that stragglers will flee for the bush." Angus grew even more serious. That's where we come in. We'll be to the northern end of the killing field and to the left as you look at it on the map...to stop any mad bastard trying to get home to mummy in the dear old village in Rhodesia.

"Also," he continued, "There will be SAS out there. Their job is to watch our backs and make this place as much as a mass grave as we can. Maximum effort, gents for maximum effect. This is scheduled to last no longer than two hours. We hit them in the morning; we want to be out by the afternoon."

There was a stunned silence in the briefing room. Then, from near the back, the stentorian voice of Corporal Josiah Innocent boomed "Bout fucking time! But why let the Scouts take the glory?"

Angus looked sharply at Josiah. He was a fine soldier, a top man in the bush. "Because they planned it, they have the go-ahead and it was their go. If you'd thought of it instead of sitting on your arse – a wildly inaccurate accusation as anyone who had been in bush with Josiah knew – it might have been ours. There's also a lot more of them than there are of us. We work together on this one and anyone who goes red-eyed on me is back to working on the motorpool." Red-eyed, they all knew, was self-explanatory. The heat of the battle, the mad rush of excitement and adrenalin had caused more than one soldier to try and win the battle single-handedly. Also never, he was proud to admit, among the Leopards.

"There's a full briefing at 0900 tomorrow so make sure your kit is right, We go in weapons heavy and nothing else." He smiled at Josiah. "You're the exception...you can bring your Bible. One more thing, gentlemen, we go pre-dawn the next day. The Scouts are driving in, we're 'chuting.."

A mock groan rose through the room. Low altitude jumps, often from no more than 300 feet, meant there was one chance of a parachute opening exactly right. Injuries were common, as were deaths, morbidly referred to as "meat packs".

"Sounds like old times," the broad Australian accent of Drew Jones cracked the silence, the comment directed at the Black American Ian Moore sitting a couple of rows in front of him. Angus had mercilessly recruited from the entire Rhodesian army for his men. The Australian and the American were both Vietnam special forces veterans, highly decorated for their work behind enemy lines and had joined the Rhodesian Light Infantry when "peace" became inevitable in that particular hellhole. Both were highly respected in the Leopards through their trademark professionalism and if either had a complaint it was that there was not enough jungle in the largely arid Rhodesia, but in the Eastern Highlands they had come through with shining colours. Angus also had an Englishman, himself ex- SAS, a Dutchman and even a Korean – possibly the most ruthless fighters in Vietnam. All fitted in to the irregular unit as if to the manner born.

"Repeating. Our job is a blocking one, the Scouts do the major work, but with more than five thousand in there we'll have plenty of blocking to do," Angus paused. "So what the hell are you doing sitting on your arses in here?'

The Leopards quickly scattered, to assemble kit, check and recheck weapons. They did it quietly, mostly by themselves as they thought of the size of the target.

Angus retired to his office and absently-mindedly scanned the paperwork. Most of which could be left for the sergeant, he decided. For the first time since turning to base, he allowed his thoughts to drift towards Kate. That she was delectable was an undisputed, desirable totally inadequate a description. It was complicated and complex, yes. She was a free spirit, certainly. But for the first time in his life, Angus felt a little of his depth, out of the comfort zone which had seen him largely sail though it all, with only a few minor skirmishes - largely caused by growing up with parents who encouraged a certain wild streak in him. Childish pranks, mainly.

He stretched and ruffled his hair. Never before had he given the keys to his flat to a girl and certainly never the keys to the Jag. But then never before had he felt a longing for another person that a night on the town and a night with a temporary right female company had not assuaged.

Angus grinned to himself. Then caught sight of himself in the small mirror on the wall. It abruptly brought him back to the present. "I'm no use to anyone if I moon around while we're on a major mission," he silently admonished himself. "No bloody use at all." Kate would wait, but not if he and his men didn't make it back.

Suddenly angry with himself, he slapped his Leopard beret on his head and went in search of Daniel. He found him sitting in the sunshine cleaning his weapon for the umpteenth time.

"You clean that fucking thing one more time you'll wear it out," he told Daniel, who merely glanced up from the work at hand and kept cleaning.

"Kate trouble?" he enquired artlessly. Sister Sally had kept him secretly posted on all the latest doings in *that* particular affair. Daniel himself wholeheartedly approved and had been fascinated by the taming of the lion. For the first time Angus had found himself in the situation where he couldn't do as he pleased when he pleased. Maybe the spoilt boy was finally growing up, Daniel had privately sniggered to himself, while maintaining a straight face through it all. But this opportunity was just too good to miss with his oldest friend.

"Ah...bugger it Daniel," Angus sheepishly replied. "No Kate trouble...just no Kate. Work to do, man." As much as he hated to admit it, particularly to himself, Daniel could always see straight though him and cut to the core of the matter. His own perspective on things *was* changing, he realised. Previously he could go off on a mission like switching off one light and turning on another. A job to do, hopefully survive and do it successfully and move on without remorse to the next challenge. Now, he had become almost instinctively more circumspect, a tad more careful in his approach. He as yet didn't quite catch on that most of his men were grateful for the slight change. He shook his head as if to cast off water spray. There was no place for second thoughts on a battlefield.

"If you're all squared away, how about tennis?" No booze before the battle was the rule. There was also no room for hangovers out in the bush, although more than a few on his men fortified themselves with ghanga, the wicked weed of Africa. He knew about it, did not approve, but left each man to find his own measure of courage. So far it had worked well. Out of the original fifty Leopards, he had lost just three in the bush. All had died courageously and all had been posthumously honoured. On the credit side of the ledger, the Leopards were officially marked down for more than five hundred kills. Given that the kill to wounded ratio was generally recognised at two-to-one, they had inflicted a tremendous amount of damage to the terrorist cause.

The Leopards had been in action for just a year now...he and Kate had been in action, he grinned to himself, for just on nine months with no signs of the whole affair abating. Indeed, it was growing stronger with every passing day, Angus reflected.

"Tennis it is," Daniel grinned.

Chapter Seven

The Colonel burst through the gate of the tennis court in a high state of agitation. Not an excitable man – even his mother called him dour – he was visibly upset. Angus and Daniel let the ball drop to the court and went to him.

"How ready are the Leopards?" he demanded. Angus blinked. This was not the Colonel they knew.

"Raring to go," he replied. "Totally ready." The Colonel sagged a little with relief. "New orders as of now," he said. "Your involvement with the Scouts mission is cancelled and I want you on the choppers in thirty minutes. There has been a major massacre at Chomle village...the bastards seems to have killed everybody. Men, women, children, babies...oh my God!"

Angus and Daniel raced for their quarters. Within fifteen minutes, such had been the state of readiness, the Leopards were fully packed, weapons-heavy and heading for the airstrip, where the helicopters waited. Running with them, of course, was Dog, the biggest Rhodesian Ridgeback Angus had ever seen, probably crossed with a German shepherd? Angus had personally selected the name, rejecting suggestions such as "Killer and Fang" from the others. In the heat of battle, he'd reasoned, calling "Dog" was a lot easier for all concerned. Dog, who had one day just appeared on base and wandered around, dispelling any offers of friendship from all and sundry, had found Angus eventually and formed a particular attachment with him. It might have been the way the massive creature evoked no fear from the man sitting in the sun quietly drinking a cold beer. It might have been that the dozing Angus had cocked one eye at him, shown no fear and without haste reached out a hand and scratched him behind the ears. Within a minute Dog had found what he didn't know he was looking for. But he knew he had found it now.

The only drawback was that if one of the troopers called another a dog, or mentioned he had a 'dog of a day', he would find Dog's legs curled around his neck and a big, wet slobbering tongue expressing affection. Dog was also a seasoned paratrooper, having jumped on several occasions into hot zones, although with the aid of a static-line 'chute. High altitude, low openings, known as Halos, were however beyond him.

As they sprinted to the waiting choppers, he saw the Colonel was already there, visibly pleased with the quick response, reminding himself once again just why the Leopards were such a crack outfit. There was never any mucking around. He just had to give them the job and point them in the right direction.

"There were two survivors who were outside the village at the time and saw everything," he said. "They hid and ran to the nearest village." He paused. Apparently there were around three dozen gooks. They killed everything they could find...even the dogs and chickens."

Angus nodded. It was not new, but that never made it less distressing. Innocent people, living innocent lives. No wonder, he irrelevantly thought, two-thirds of the Rhodesian army were black. These were their kinfolk being slaughtered. Even the Charlie Tangos – communist terrorists - admitted, that in their training camps in Tanzania, Zambia and Mozambique, that they were trained to believe this was not a racial war, a black-versus-white, but a communism versus capitalism fight. To the death. Unfortunately, white farmers and black villagers were often the easiest targets once they had crossed the border back into Rhodesia.

The Leopards were loading onto the choppers. Angus turned to the Colonel. "By the way," he said. "How many Scouts are going on that mission?"

The Colonel blinked. "Seventy-two" he said. "Against how many?" Angus enquired. "Five thousand," was the answer.

"Should be a stroll in the park," Angus grinned and ran to the last waiting chopper. He leapt on board and almost instantly they were airborne, in a gut-wrenching power swoop take off, snaking off to the port side at maximum revs.

It was just over 100 kilometres to Chomle and at full attack speed the ground flashed past them. Angus looked across at Daniel and caught his eye. No words were needed; they knew each other so well a glance was as good as a full conversation. They knew the drill, get there quickly, establish a trail out left by the terrs and get cracking. If the trail was obvious, the helicopters would be standing by. If not, they had some of the best trackers in the country, including Daniel.

However the best tracker they had was crouched into a corner of the 'copter, a young man from Daniel's leased farm. He was barely eighteen, a skinny lean boy. He was certainly no soldier, but in Daniel's words the young Joseph could track an ant across a river. Angus used him sparingly and often reluctantly, but he had never seen Joseph lose a track.

The terrs would be followed until the bitter end.

Smoke gave away the location of Chomle village long before they could see it. As the choppers landed, the smell of smoke was tinged with something far more sinister, the coppery smell of blood and the reek of guts.

Angus took one cursory look around the remains of the village. More than two hundred were dead, he estimated. Many were in grotesque poses, shot at point blank range by AK47s, bayoneted as they lay, dismembered as in some ghoulish nightmare, except for the limbless children who were no part of anybody's dream. They were real. Heads hacked off, arms and legs cut through with mindless savagery.

Dead dogs and chickens added to the misery. Nothing in the village stirred, except for a few still smouldering huts which were collapsing. And above it all the terrible buzzing of feasting flies. Angus glanced skywards. Sure even then, there were vultures circling. Soon, hyena would cringe towards the carnage.

One of Angus' men, Danni de Vies, was being violently sick. Danni was always violently sick in such circumstances and nobody thought any less of him. He was expressing what they all felt. He was perhaps one of the bravest to be able to show his emotions both Angus and Daniel had always thought.

Angus felt the murderous rage mounting in his men. That was good. It built the adrenalin and sharpened the senses, as long as it was kept under control. He found Daniel, who had been checking for a trail out.

"Very clearly heading for the border and home to Mozambique," Daniel said. They left about five hours ago, judging from the spoor. Angus cursed. If they had shotgunned, split up into smaller groups and taken different routes away the task of tracking became almost impossible. They could find themselves hunting down one man.

"Choppers now," he roared to his men, detailing eight, two squads, to stay behind. The clean-up soldiers would be here in a while, but for the moment the vultures and hyenas could fuck off. Angus knew they were an essential part of African life, but what had been human beings, with hopes, dreams and life were definitely off the menu today.

In the lead chopper, Daniel and another expert tracker, John Chetwe, sat on the doorsill, their feet on the landing skids and craned outwards and forward, each held by their webbing by the man behind. At fifty feet above ground at more than a hundred knots it was perilous work, particularly for the pilots, who had to react instantly to signals as well as avoiding the occasional tree or stone outcrop.

Daniel straightened and gave the cut-off sign. Angus immediately realised why. They had left the semi-arid land and were entering into the more forested area leading to the highlands.

He estimated they had covered about thirty kilometres and did the math in his head. Assuming the terrs were in a hurry, which they would be, they would be sprinting the first few kilometres before settling into a jog-trot which would steadily eat up the miles. But, then again, he reasoned, after such a slaughter they would be reckless, drunk with the madness of it, possibly drunk in the first place or high as kites on ganga. Much more likely, he thought. These were not professional soldiers, but more a motley collection where battle-ready meant being able to stand and shoot. Exceptions were there, of course, but exceptions were the exception. His reasoning was that professionals would have done the job without the mutilations. But then again, maybe they were looking for the horror factor.

So, he calculated, in five hours at best they would have covered forty to fifty kilometres. More realistically, just over thirty. They had left a spoor a baby could follow; backing his belief these were not crack troops. Angus and his men had not overflown them, so the bandits were ahead, just how far ahead remained to be seen. He checked with the pilots before jumping out of the chopper. They had come twenty-seven kilometres, so by Angus' reckoning they were between five and ten kilometres behind. Sooner or later, the terrs would stop to rest, exhausted by their work and doubly tired once the adrenalin of the slaughter wore off. They would collapse like tired dogs around a camp fire. Or so he was gambling. If they were top of the range terrs they would keep going until they reached safety and could be many more kilometres ahead. Angus firmly shut the thought from his mind. Political protest was one thing. Deliberately dismembering babies and pregnant women quite another.

The Leopards fanned out into a tight reverse arrow formation, with Daniel and John at the forefront, each Leopard now capable of covering another and attacking forward or to the side. They went at Leopard pace, a steady trot which would chew ten kilometres an hour through most terrain. More deadly, though, they were quiet. Dead branches were leapt over, foliage from trees and scrub avoided. It had been said in the past the loudest thing about a

Leopard advance was the sound of their breathing. They moved like the deadly cat whose name they bore.

Daniel and John were following a clearly-defined spoor. There had been no attempt at anti-tracking, no effort to disguise where they were headed. Angus puzzled over for a moment, and then cleared his head of the matter. Why would they be furtive? They had attacked a reasonably isolated village, destroyed everything, believed there were no witnesses and were now headed for sanctuary.

They didn't know about the fast-response unit called the Leopards, or if they did assumed wrongly the Leopards were too far away to be of any threat. They obviously had no idea that the Leopards were about the bore right up their arses and give them the reaming of their soon-to-end lives.

Daniel suddenly gave the cut-off signal again, a different one this time which meant "contact imminent". Angus smiled to himself. His gamble may have paid off. They could have crept through the bush at snails' pace and followed the terrs all the way into Mozambique before catching up with them. This way could lead to instant justice. The Leopards now were in a frozen position on the ground, each man with his weapon at the ready.

He looked enquiringly at Daniel, who pointed to the tracks and held up the fingers of one hand. Five. Five minutes behind. Angus signalled to the four closest men to him to close up. They in turn signalled to their nearest neighbours, who passed on the message until silently the group was in a neatly-bunched formation. Thirty two of the most formidable soldiers in Rhodesia. Dog sniffed the air and raised his front leg, pointing in a specific direction. One of Angus' shortcomings was he had little sense of smell, a personal failure he wryly reflected had led to more than one "discussion" with Kate over brands of perfume he had bought her. Essence of Dried Leprous Camel Dung had been one description from her. He brought himself back to reality. Different men had different ways of dealing with the stress of the immediate future. In Angus' case he allowed himself a five second fantasy, which in the now distant past had involved booze and broads.

John, with his exceptional sense of smell, made the sign for smoke. Five minutes ahead the bastards were cooking up supper, or preparing a bonfire to ward off the chills of the night. Angus smiled grimly. Arrogant swine. He glanced at the sky. It was last light, the sudden twilight of the deep southern hemisphere, the evening star already rising.

He made a decision. Five minutes ahead probably translated to about a kilometre, about as far as a nose like John's could discern the smoke. He made the sign and the Leopards crept forward, all now on high alert. Angus wondered for a moment whether the terrs would have posted sentries. He thought it unlikely, given their certainty they were safe, but had absolute faith in his men that any found would be disposed of – silently.

By now even he could smell the smoke. About one hundred metres, he estimated and made more handsigns. The bulk of the Leopards froze, while he, Daniel, John, Dog and two others soundlessly made their way forward.

Dog gave a soft growl. The terrs were in a clearing, Angus saw. A large fire was burning brightly, and exhausted-looking men were slumped around it. There had been no sentries. Angus counted. More than the estimated three dozen, he saw at once. Perhaps some had stayed out of the village to catch any who tried to flee. That made sense. With a feeling of bitter nausea he noticed that many were coated in dried blood. He counted again, to make sure. Yes, there were forty-five, dressed in the traditional terr uniforms of worn-out denims and sandshoes, armed with AK47s. Many of which had simply been dumped on the ground.

He motioned to John to return and bring the men up. Silently through the now-night they arrived and Angus dispersed them into a semi-circle around the terr group. The terrs themselves were surprisingly quiet, with just muttered conversation as they devoured rations. There were just the usual sounds of Africa Comes to Life at Night as the nocturnal animals woke. In the far distance a lion exercised his vocal chords.

Angus checked again to ensure his men were in place. That he couldn't see them didn't surprise him – he would have returned-to-unit any man visible. It was time. The signal to open fire would come from Angus, from his first shot.

He sighted a man who looked a likely leader, stronger and more robust than the rest, with an unmistakable air of authority. He was haranguing a junior soldier and Angus didn't need to be a lip-reader to understand what he was saying. He could hear every syllable.

Angus carefully took aim and squeezed the trigger. The leader's head exploded. There was a stunned silence among the terrs for a moment, and then all hell broke loose as a barrage of bullets poured into the makeshift camp.

Thirty two M16s, capable of firing seven hundred rounds a minute didn't leave anything standing. Within two minutes it was all over. What was left was piles of shredded bush meat. Angus felt the vultures and hyenas would enjoy the feast. He hoped, cynically, they weren't poisoned by it.

The gruesome task now began of sifting through the bodies, looking for any damning documents. Angus personally took on the leader he had killed, the shot through the head leaving the body intact, with the row of cheap pens demarking rank and, a gold mine, papers indicating the purpose of their mission – and several other names of nearby villages. More importantly, to Angus' mind, there was also a list of white farms which nestled against the highlands, mainly growing tea. It was puzzling to him. Had this group meant to move on to other targets and were merely taking a rest while the heat from the village died down? Judging from their lack of rations and depleted ammunition, probably not.

Angus suddenly cursed and in his own mind whacked himself on the forehead, with a swear word or two gathering puzzled looks from those nearby. Of course not! They were waiting to be resupplied! Another group, this time lackeys and those judged unfit for military service would be trudging towards them with fresh supplies – ammunition the most vital, food and perhaps even clothes. He pondered a moment and called Daniel over.

"These pricks were going to be resupplied," he explained his reasoning to Daniel, who nodded in agreement. "The question is, do we wait for them to resupply us, or pass it on?" Angus was quite aware the Leopards had come in weapons-heavy with little food except for emergency rations. That, in itself, was of little concern. Each and every one of them could live off the land for an indefinite period. Their problem, ironically, was ammo.

"Organise a drop?" Daniel suggested. Angus had already thought of that, but he occasionally needed psychological back-up and he trusted Daniel like no other man. A drop had been his thoughts exactly. He called to Ralph, who had the burden of carrying the radio and told him to raise Bulawayo. While he waited as Ralph rigged the aerial, he looked around his men with pride. The Leopards had come though again, utter professionalism and absolute sheer dispassionate performance. This night's work is going to cost me more than a few beers, he grinned. Dog particularly enjoyed a couple of pints.

"Colonel for you, Angus," Ralph said, handing Angus the handset. Angus quickly described the conflict, the outcome, then the probability of a resupply unit making its way towards them. He kept it short and coded in such a way that only the Colonel would understand what he was proposing. "Forty five expired falcons and mother geese on way. Tea is risky." would have made little sense to anyone else. Although working a highly restricted, and secret, frequency, there was always the chance the radio had been compromised. It had happened many times in the rest of the army, sometimes with tragic results.

"Negative," the Colonel replied, to Angus' surprise. "Come home. Out." And that was it. "Now what," Angus asked Daniel, "do you suppose that was about?" He wasn't unduly perturbed, but it seemed a rich picking was to be ignored. He pondered some more, lighting a cigarette and letting the smoke do the thinking. The Colonel, occasionally, moved in mysterious ways.

"Well he's not going to tell you over the fucking radio, is he?" Daniel replied.

Chapter Eight

The problem was, Angus wryly but realistically thought, there
was no mention of just how they could come home, immediately
as per the colonel's orders. There were no choppers this time – the
Rhodesian military were desperately short. So walk back, it was,
to the nearest point they could find transport. He consulted the
map. Umtali was the closest town, about 25km to the north and
back in predominantly Shona country. And, Angus remembered,
at Umtali there was an army barracks. It had grown out of all
proportion since the threats to the Highlands grow more brutal. In
fact, Angus recalled, it was the home of 4RR, part of the vaunted
Rhodesian Regiment which itself dated back to 1898. Where there
were big army barracks, there were trucks – trucks which could
be commandeered to transport the Leopards back to Bulawayo.

It took almost a full day to reach the outskirts of Umtali,
where as in so many African towns they first passed the slums
suburbs, in this case the flea-market, fruit stall and tin shanties of
Sakubva before making their way into Umtali proper, regarded by
many as the most beautiful of all Rhodesian towns and a popular
place for honeymooners and holiday-makers before the war
intensified. It, ironically, was also called the Gateway to the Sea,
as the main transit point to Beira, on the coast of Mozambique.
Those particular days were long gone.

Angus and the Leopards were oblivious to the charms. The
bought fruit and bottles of iced beer and they made their way

through the city, quaffing them as they made their way to the barracks, which were protected by heavy barbed and link wire fortifications, as well as watchtowers. The sentries looked them in askance. The Leopards wore no insignia of rank and carried no identification. But the obvious European element in the group and Angus' clipped educated Rhodesian accent carried the day and they were directed to the CO's office.

The sign on the door read "Colonel John Roberts". Angus almost laughed out loud. It couldn't be! He burst in through the door without knocking, to find a huge gorilla of a man hunched over a series of maps. Roberts glared up at the rude interruption.

"Bobbie you son of a hyena!" Angus roared. "They finally got you doing some soldiering work!" It was a grossly unfair accusation, as both of them knew, but Roberts was still coming to terms with the wild apparition standing before him with a grin from ear to ear and pounding his back with gusto.

"Dunrow...?" he finally managed. "Angus?" then he too broke into festivities. Many had been the time the Roberts/Dunrow team had wreaked havoc in Bulawayo and Salisbury nightspots. It was said you could tell how much fun Roberts/Dunrow had the night before by both the wake of broken tables – and hearts – and the length of time it took either to be able to mumble the slightest word in the coming days.

"What the *fuck* are you doing here, man?" Roberts finally enquired, fishing a bottle of Jameson's from his drawer and pouring two healthy measures. Angus quickly filled him in on the hunt and culls and tactfully brought the conversation around to the need for transport.

Roberts waved airily: "Take a couple of trucks, my boys can bring them back. But it's too late now, so set off tomorrow." He grinned slyly at Angus. "Give us time to properly catch up and you and your boys can have a proper braai tonight. Give them a decent reward, eh?" Angus agreed wholeheartedly. If the Colonel had thought it urgent to get back, he would have dispatched the choppers.

"Anything you need from Bulawayo?" Angus asked. Resupply was a bane of Rhodesian army life. With the heavy sanctions imposed from countries around the work, including former allies Britain and America, many important items were like hen's teeth, which had led to the growing reliance on South Africa, itself becoming a global outcast through, in Angus' eyes, its destructive apartheid policies.

Roberts shook his head. "We've the beer, the boys and the best morale around. We only have to stroll out of the camp to make contact and so far the count is baddies very many versus good guys very few." He relaxed visibly. "We'll make do Angus."

Even so, Angus privately vowed he would send some cases of liquor back for Roberts' personal stock. He knew how lonely it could be at the top. He took a slug of the drink Roberts had poured and for the first time in many days relaxed.

The truck journey out the next day was a jolting, bone-jarring reminder of the undying friendships sworn between the Leopards and the 4RR as the braai had sizzled on the barbeques and the cases of beer were emptied. Several Leopards had forgone sleep altogether and eyes the colour of the previous night's sunset greeted the new dawn through ferocious scowls. Angus smiled. He and John Roberts had conducted their own, more private and circumspect celebration, though Angus admitted to himself the dull thump behind his eyes was probably not due to a bad ice cube mixed into their drinks. Dog slept heavily, his massive frame spread comfortably over Angus' legs. He had consumed more than a couple of pints. He was also adept at furtively pinching bottled beer and slurping the contents.

It was five hours back to Bulawayo, a time when most of the Leopards dozed, but ready to come to instant alert if they ran into trouble. But it was a beautiful day, crisp in the cloudless weather and the trucks made good time, slowing only for the occasional farm truck or one of the lumbering Kudus – the heavily fortified, uniquely-designed fighting vehicles designed to take out ambushes with awesome firepower and to disperse the devastating effects of land mines laid on the roads. A Rhodesian invention, the principle of which spread throughout the world, in was just one of many vehicles modified to help ensure safe travel around the country. Perhaps the most ungainly was one based on a Volkswagen, with elongated "legs" attached to the wheels, where passengers sat high, and hopefully safe, above the land mine explosions.

The Colonel greeted them home with a "well done" and told them to stand down after the compulsory debriefing. He turned to Angus and Daniel and indicated with a tilt of his head a private meeting was in order. The two men followed him to his office.

"What now," Angus asked the Colonel. "I ask the question rhetorically, of course. You said get back here immediately."

The Colonel smiled. "We already had the list of targets from other sources and the area is crawling with troopies and the Light Infantry. You were surplus to requirements. We also didn't have a place available for a drop – they're all committed to this mission."

Angus looked at him mollified. "My men have been going flat out for months now. They won't show it, but the signs are there," he replied honestly. "Shakes, short nerves, perhaps a tad trigger-happy. They need furlough, time to get back and see their families and friends and hose the horrors out for a while. They're good, but they are buggered."

"And you and Daniel?" the Colonel enquired with an arched eyebrow. Angus looked him directly in the eye. "Yes, us also," he quietly said.

The Colonel toyed with a pencil on his desk. "I'm been slowly coming to the same conclusion," he said. "You both look shattered...no don't argue," he severely cut across the protest forming on Angus' lips. "After the debrief the Leopards disappear for a month. No-one will know where you are going – dress it up as secret training if you like." The Colonel was nothing if not perspective. There are just so many times you can send a thoroughbred out to race before he tumbles at the first corner.

"So" he smiled. "Bugger off."

Chapter Nine

The Leopards dispersed out of the camp within hours, some driving, others cadging lifts, taking trains and busses. One thing Angus wasn't concerned about was security for the men on leave. Unlike other elements of the military, the Leopards shunned publicity and to Angus' knowledge no picture of any of the men – himself excepted – had ever appeared in any publication. Other units had found out the hard way, men going back to their homelands on leave, recognised by the dissidents and murdered. Even the famed Selous Scouts had lost four members in that fashion, before the shutters had been well and truly lowered and bolted.

But it had proved impossible to keep the existence of the Leopards a total secret, particularly with every mounting success and the rumour mill working overtime. Angus had been elected as the spokesman, a job he hated, with the obligatory photographs appearing in the Press. Angus mentally shrugged it off. Nobody was likely to bump him off at HillView Farm, or in the main streets of Bulawayo.

However, now he had a dilemma on his hands and for the first time in weeks, time to face it head-on. As much as he disliked it, the sheer intensity of the work had kept him from Kate for longer and longer periods. Snatched phone calls between missions had been about the limit of things. Angus hoped he wasn't imagining demons, but Kate had seemed to grow more distant with every call.

In fact her last contact with him had ended abruptly with: "So, you're off again then...well, good luck." Good luck? Angus swore to himself. That was the worst hex of all. Wisely, he had not shared the conversation with Daniel, who – good Christian he may be – retained many Matabele superstitions.

And now looking in the mirror as he shaved the three week growth off, he was no oil painting either. Deep lines furrowed his brow, his eyes appeared to have become almost devoid of emotion, pebble-like. The 1000-metre stare, they called it. Bringing the razor to his chin, he noticed his hand was trembling and he swore as he cut himself. His back was bent from the pain of the often inhumanly-heavy packs and weapons they were forced to carry, his legs were a mess of scars and a couple of festering sores from insect bites. His left collarbone was agony when he tried to lift his arm above his shoulder after a slip on rocky terrain and a perilous tumble into a shallow ravine.

He took further stock of Captain Angus Dunrow. A scarecrow would have been ashamed. He was finding it increasingly difficult to control his calm and had shouted at an innocent batman who left a mark on his dress boots. Worse, a rift had subtly developed between he and Daniel. On hearing the leave order, Daniel had simply mounted his BSA motorbike and roared out of camp, still filthy dirty, headed for home. Angus thought of Daniel. Grey beneath his black exterior, also shaking and listless in command. They had all been to hell together too often.

Angus had retired to the officers' mess with a bottle of gin, which he nursed between both hands to prevent spillage and guzzled it, glaring menacingly at any who attempted to approach him.

Kate, meantime he brooded, was comfortably ensconced in the Bulawayo apartment, driving the Jag. The horrors of the bush war had as yet barely touched the city, apart from the horror roll of injured arriving at the hospital. Angus, he realised in a moment of sobriety, Angus himself was being terribly unfair. She was trying to tend to the messes they were medivacing and trucking into the hospital from the bush.

73

He finished shaving, looked at his reflection, then anger boiled over. "Fuck it!" he screamed and smashed his fist into the mirror. It shattered into a myriad of pieces and Angus stupidly looked at his hand. Badly cut, but he didn't feel a thing. He looked back at the broken mirror, at the pieces of jagged reflections that now appeared. Yes, that was now him, he thought.

A shattered man in a shattered war in a shattered country.

He shook himself like a Labrador shaking off water after a swim and made his way to the first aid hut for attention for his injuries. His first attempt at conversing with the orderly came out slurred. Jack Thompson had seen it all before, as an Australian medic in Vietnam, but the shock of seeing the Golden Boy in such a state rendered him speechless. Quickly, efficiently and practically he bound Angus' more superficial wounds without questions or comment.

Thompson then fished into a private cupboard and handed Angus a vial of pills. "These will help, mate," he said. Angus stared stupidly in turn first at the vial and then at Thompson. Not trusting himself to speak, he nodded and walked out into the sunshine.

So where to now, he thought. He couldn't hang around camp, as the only Leopard. He could go back to HillView and hope for Matilda's love to patch him back together. Or he could do what he had done a thousand times in the bush – deliberately face his fears - and go into Bulawayo.

He dressed casually and took the Landrover from its shed, motoring sedately out of the camp and not letting the beast have its head until he was on the sealed road. In just minutes he pulled up outside his apartment and let himself in. Joshua, as always was waiting, there was cold beer in the fridge, but something seemed amiss. There was no feminine clutter, either in the main room, or in the main bedroom, Joshua had remained silent until now.

"The Nkosana moved away," he sorrowfully told Angus. "She was crying, but three weeks ago she returned to the nurses's kraal."

Angus felt gutshot. All gone, for what? So he and the Leopards could be glory boys in the bush, he bitterly thought. He briefly thought of the gun cabinet, securely locked in the special room, then immediately discarded the idea which had half formed in his mind. That way was the coward's way. He opened a bottle of Lion, sipped, then violently threw it at the nearest bin, still foaming.

There was only one way to deal with this, for better or worse. He checked his watch, just coming up to three o'clock. Wearily, he rose and took the Rover keys from his pocket and made it down the stairs.

Just after three, Angus hid the Rover behind a convenient tree and took at seat on the park bench on the lawn fronting the hospital entrance. He had no plan what to say, how to act or where to begin. He wasn't sure he had the courage to even face Kate.

Just fifteen minutes later Kate emerged, with several other nurses. She looked worn, Angus immediately saw and had lost her colour. Even her hair looked drab and there was no sparkle in her step or conversation.

She glanced over the lawn and seemed to ignore the figure slumped on the bench, taking three more steps before coming to an abrupt halt and looking again. Tentatively, she broke from the rest of the group and approached. With effort, Angus heaved himself to his feet, so just two metres separated them. She looked searchingly at Angus and tears began to flow down her face.

"Oh, Angus...," she whispered. "What have they done to you?" She moved slowly to him, never taking her eyes from the ravaged face looking down at her. Kate slid slowly into Angus's awkward embrace, her arms right around him and now the tears began in earnest. It was only when she felt moisture on her own hair that she turned tear-stained eyes upwards. Angus was crying also, deep-wracking sobs which were all the more dreadful because of his silence.

She spied the Landrover and half-hauled Angus towards it, jumping over the side and kicking open the passenger door. Kate pushed him into the left hand seat, where he sat listlessly, hunched over and showing no interest in the surroundings, locked in his own tortured world. Dog gave Kate a quick slobber of affection then lay down in the rear compartment. She drove slowly to the apartment, all the time casting anxious looks at him.

The change was unbelievable, she thought. The last time she had seen Angus, she realised now almost three months ago, he had been taut with nervous energy, a little too loud and almost rushed in their love-making. That had been for just three days and he had been called back for another emergency. But at least he had left her with a smile, a kiss and a promise to be back soon.

But since then there had just been the perfunctory phone calls, often cut short. Kate, in turn, had increasingly felt cut adrift. She initially felt selfish, for there were many other women in her position with husbands and lovers caught up fighting in the war. She also saw, often on a daily basis, the terribly maimed men being emergency-transferred to her ward, heard their groans and tears and nightmares.

It had been their nightmares which had proved the turning point. Kate began to have them herself, alone in the apartment, but it was not her in the thick of the action, it was Angus. How many nights she had woken screaming, she wondered. Only to cry until dawn, until it was time for a new shift.

There had been a handsome new doctor come onto the ward. Cheerful, confident and caring, able to be alternatively jolly and bully many of the wounded into the rehabilitation process. "So you've only got one leg," he said to one man. "That's why God gave you two. We'll make you a new one and you can go and kick another mine without worrying about it." It was grim but effective humour and many of the wounded responded well.

So had Kate and for a wild moment she had considered setting her sail for him. But the spectre of Angus and all he had been hung over her. And the doctor had started hearing the legend of Angus Dunrow and Kate's connection to him and that was that, much had to admit to herself, to her own relief.

She pulled into the apartment's garage and killed the motor. The door leading to the stairs opened and Joshua appeared, as if summoned. Wordlessly, he slung his powerful arm around Angus and half-dragged him from the Rover and up the steps to the main living area. There a further surprise waiting.

Jonathon and Elizabeth Dunrow were there, Elizabeth sitting nervously in an easy chair and Jonathon pacing the floor, his brow creased with worry lines.

Kate tried without success to hide her shock. Jonathon was crucial to the Rhodesian Government and must have taken the family's private plane to fly down from Salisbury. Kate remembered also that urgent crisis talks were currently being held.

"My God Angus," he started, and then strode to Joshua's support as Angus began to slide to the floor. "Quick," he ordered Kate. "Get me Foster-Jones on the phone." Kate quailed inside. Professor James Foster-Jones was the head of the hospital, a brilliant physician with a reputation of being something of a tyrant. For a comparatively junior member of staff to ring him...

But she made the call and using the Dunrow name steered through the layers of bureaucracy till finally an abrupt "Yes" came through the earpiece. With no small measure of relief she handed the phone to Jonathon.

"James," Jonathon began without the courtesies. "Need you here, right now...I don't give a bugger about your meeting, right now and bring your bag of tricks." He reeled off the address and slammed the receiver down. He steadied for a moment and winked at Kate. "Owes me a favour or three," he explained. "Particularly in the funding department.

Joviality immediately set aside, he went to Angus' side. His son was collapsed on a sofa, but his eyes were open, albeit unfocussed.

"Too much from too few for too long," Jonathon mused, half to himself. Elizabeth was sponging Angus' brow with a cold cloth and Joshua had removed his boots. Kate hovered uncertainly. Jonathon looked over to her. "You did well," he said. "Very well. We'd heard from the Brig he was in a bad way, and then Joshua came up with the courage to contact me. Flew down immediately."

There was a ring at the door, which then opened and Professor James Foster-Jones strode in. A tall, almost cadaverous man with a pronounced stoop and reputed to never smile, he was nonetheless considered in the top two men in his field in the country. Ignoring the others he went straight to Angus.

"Yes...yes...mmm...yes...I see...yes...," he murmured as he examined Angus, finally standing up and, to Kate's surprise, ruffling Angus' hair with a friendly gesture. From his bag he produced a needle and a vial and slipped it into Angus' arm.

"Well Jon," not many people got away with calling Jonathon Jon, but Professor James Foster-Brown was obviously among the elite. "What we have here is a totally – and I mean totally – exhausted man, physically and more seriously mentally. How long has he been on this caper? Five, six years?"

"Tell me something I don't know," Jonathon snarled.

Kate suddenly saw the compassion flowing from Foster-James. "Jon, my friend, there is one cure and one cure alone. We could and will give him some mild sedatives to relax him in the short term – I just gave him one, but what he needs, what will cure him, is rest. Uninterrupted rest. No phones, no news, just rest. Take him to your farm and keep him there, under lock and key if you have to for at least two months. Under no account must he have any more stress or strain or the next time could be permanent. He may not come back."

"Will he...this time," Kate ventured. Foster-James smiled at her – another first, proving the rumours wrong, Kate irrelevantly thought.

"Yes he will, Kate," the professor announced. "Particularly with a caring, dedicated and pretty nurse like you looking out for him."

Kate felt swept up in a tumultuous wave. "Me?" She tentatively began..."but what about the hospital?"

"You are now on full-time secondment to the 23 Field Ambulance Unit, based at HillView Farm," Foster-James pronounced. "By the way, so is Sally Nkomo. From all accounts Daniel is not the best, either. The two of you are all we can spare for the 23rd, which I'll create on my return to hospital."

Chapter Ten

The procession to HillView went without hitch and at slightly a lower speed than Kate had been used to with Angus "Stirling Moss" Dunrow behind the wheel. Angus himself was in an ambulance, attached to various drips feeding vital nutrients and sedatives into his body. Kate drove the Jaguar, with Elizabeth as her passenger, and Jonathon taking charge of the LandRover.

"Been waiting to have a go at this bugger for ages," he cheerfully brushed off protests that a Minister of the Government should be more safely ensconced in the Jaguar. "Can't wait to see what Frikkie's bag of tricks has achieved. But after he had planted his foot and fishtailed down the road burning rubber from the tires, he immediately slowed with a slightly sickly expression on his face. "Bloody hell..," he mused aloud. "This thing is a beast." So more sedately, they proceeded.

The bush telegraph in Africa is phenomenal. There had been no beating of drums during the night, nor messages carried in cleft sticks. More prosaically, Joshua had probably telephoned Matilda, but it seemed the entire domestic staff and more than a few senior field workers were waiting Angus' arrival. As the stretcher was unloaded from the ambulance they began a low, harmonious humming tune, one intended to welcome the wounded warrior home and bid him speedy recovery.

Angus himself was out for the count. Kate and Elizabeth, looking down to him, imagined they could already see a slight easing of the lines on his face, while his body was not hunched anymore, but lying quite straight on his back. It had been decided that his own room was the best nursing location, so he would eventually wake to familiar surroundings. The servants had bent their backs to cleaning and sprucing up the large room, including the addition of Angus' favourite wildflowers and opening the French doors to the courtyard to allow the room to air.

Courtesy of Foster-Jones, Angus lay almost comatose for three days, sleeping the sleep of the almost-dead. Even Tom, who by cat-telepathy appeared over the courtyard wall and padded into the bedroom, slinking onto the bed and trying to raise Angus by nuzzling his head, gave up and retired to his favourite guard-lion position on the top of the wall. Dog, who had long ago grown accustomed to Tom's presence, curled up on the bedroom floor, near the door.

On the fourth day, Angus stirred and opened his eyes. The room was spinning and he felt as helpless as a kitten. But his linen was clean and freshly starched, as were the pyjamas he was wearing. He tentatively lifted his hand and felt his face. Cleanly shaved. For some time he was content to lie and bring his surroundings into some sort of order. It was his bedroom in his family house.

He craned his head to see though the French doors, through which a gentle warm veldt breeze was blowing. For a moment he attempted to untangle the issues which had brought him here, but was rewarded with an instant piercing headache. Settling back on the pillows, Angus again tried to collect his thoughts. But there was just a blackness, a jumble of extraordinary, non-connected thoughts. He gave up and almost as suddenly the headache moderated.

Okay, Dunrow, he realised. You're home. That means you're safe. The fresh linen, the shaved face means you have been cared for...Matilda, it came to him. That was her name. A lame chuckle arose from within him. This was a long way from a scorpion bite in a boot. It must have been the faint chuckle which did it, because suddenly there was a huge lion jumping on the bed, the yellow eyes just centimetres from Angus' own as if the magnificent creature was conducting his own medical examination. A dinner-plate sized paw landed on Angus' shoulder and it was as much as he could do not to wince. Black-blue bruises were still resplendent there. Dog sat and rested his head on Angus' pillow.

But Tom was satisfied the patient was on the mend. He sat and opened the huge mouth with a roar which had the tame gazelles outside the fences bolting for cover. It also had another, more gratifying effect. Into the room burst Jonathon, Elizabeth, Kate and, waddling in the rear, Matilda.

"My God, you're awake," Jonathon exclaimed. "Bloody Foster-Jones said you'd be out for a week!" As far as opening conversation gambits went, it perhaps lacked a touch of tact, but the glistening in the corner of his father's eyes belied the rough sentiment. Not so for Elizabeth, Kate and Matilda. They all had tears pouring down their faces.

"Oh Angus...I thought we'd lost you," Elizabeth managed, smoothing his tangled hair. To have seen her son near death's door had come close to breaking her heart and she had managed to sleep only in brief snatches.

Matilda had no such inhibitions. She smothered Angus to her bosom. "Angie, Angie...Angie," she repeated.

Kate had dried her tears and now took charge. "Angus, you're a very sick man. Complete bed rest now for the rest of the week and then we'll start trying to get you mobile again," she matter-of-factly told him. Her eyes now displayed no emotion apart from professional concern. Angus looked at her in confusion and suddenly the incident of the park bench came back to him.

He matched Kate's expression with his own, a face of grim determination. "Bed rest be buggered," he said and attempted to rise. He barely made it to a sitting position before waves of dizziness and nausea overcame him and he slumped back to the pillow. "Perhaps as you say then, Sister," he muttered with ill-concealed frustration.

Kate ushered the rest from the room, including Dog, shooed Tom back to the courtyard and perched on the edge of Angus' bed. "You're here for two months," she began. "And I have been seconded for that time to bring you back to health."

"Two months!" Angus exploded, though weakly. "What the hell?"

"Two months," Kate firmly reiterated. "And Sally is with Daniel for that time, also."

Daniel! Angus felt a stab of guilt. All he remembered was Daniel riding straight out from the gates of the Bulawayo camp. Kate brought him up to date, carefully and concisely. It seemed that Daniel had briefly stopped at his farmhouse, loaded his horse with supplies and disappeared. A full-scale search of his farm and also of HillView property had failed to find any trace until an alert tracker had noticed a wisp of smoke from a hidden crevasse and come across Daniel, lying unconscious near a pool of stagnant water. They had fetched him in on a stretcher on the back of a farm truck and even now he lay, as Angus was lying, being tended back to life.

"Christ!" Angus muttered. "What have we done?" Kate slipped another sedative needle into his arm and with moments Angus was asleep again. She tucked the sheet to his chin and for a moment her stern expression faltered. Bloody Angus, bloody Daniel, bloody Leopards, she angrily thought, then made her way back to the family gathered in the easy room.

"Sorry about that," Kate said, suddenly feeling weak. Jonathon was quickly at her side and sat her in one of the over-stuffed armchairs, pouring her a strong medicinal brandy, which Kate swallowed in one hit. A little colour returned to her face.

"You may think I was tough with him then. I was. But with men in general, and in particular men like Angus, there's no room for pandering. He'll get better, I can almost guarantee that – certainly physically – but his mind will take much, much longer. He was as close to a total breakdown as any man I've seen."

"Is he out of the danger zone?" Jonathon artlessly enquired. He had been handling affairs of state via telephone hook-up and also sleeping when a brief opportunity presented itself.

"Far from it, Mr Dunrow," Kate replied. "But with proper care he has every chance." Jonathon nodded. "It's Jonathon, Kate," his smile was every bit as warm as Angus' she realised. "But I must get back to Salisbury. Elizabeth?" The question directed to his wife, as politically astute as he in many regards.

"I think I shall stay on for the time being," Elizabeth replied softly. "He may need his mother."

Jonathon accepted the decision without ranquor. It was what he had expected. For too long the family had been torn apart by this bloody war and perhaps now it was time for some start at rebuilding. He strode to the phone and ordered a helicopter pickup back to his plane waiting at Bulawayo. By evening he would be back in Salisbury.

Jonathon was a torn man. As a member of the War Cabinet he knew how vital the Leopards had become, in their secret, dirty war. The results, although highly classified, were remarkable, rivalling and in many cases exceeding those from the Selous Scouts and SAS itself. But as a parent he now had seen first-hand the terrible consequences on the soldiers themselves. First Angus, then Daniel, whom he had always regarded as a surrogate son, albeit of a slightly less fashionable hue. But then, there were forty-eight others. Jonathon vowed he would track down the rest of those men, now also on leave and judge their ability to go on. Any found suffering from what was now tentatively being labelled post-traumatic stress syndrome by the headshrinkers in the wake of the Vietnam War would be immediately returned to less arduous duties – or ordered to remain home and organise small bands of resistance in their homelands and around their farms. That, Jonathon thought with a small degree of satisfaction as he jumped aboard the helicopter, could be the next best answer.

And that indeed, he mused as they became airborne, could hold the very key to Angus' future. As a father, with wide-ranging influence and as a highly-influential member of the Government, he could easily block Angus' return to active service and particularly exposure to Leopard command. But he knew such a pre-emptive course would backfire. Angus was capable of deep-seated rebellion – one such episode had once left father and son without words or acknowledgement for each other for the best part of a full year.

The Leopards would go on, with adequate reinforcements, Jonathon decided. Angus would be dangled a carrot, with a suitable promotion, as an adviser. But the larger prize would be the chance to organise small quick-response crews to repulse attempted terrorist attacks. Could work, Jonathon mused...but nothing would be put in motion for the next two months. First, he, Elizabeth and Matilda needed Angus back. He chuckled, attracting a puzzled glance from the pilot.

In many African households, the Black servants became part of the family. Life at HillView without Matilda would be unthinkable.

Jonathon mused more as the chopper began its descent into Bulawayo. Kate? He'd been in no doubt they had been smitten with each other and had tacitly given his whole-hearted blessing. But he'd seen the look in Kate's eyes at the farm and realised there were many rocks and hidden eddies swirling under the surface of that particular stream of romance. Mentally, he shrugged. What would work out would work out...or not.

Chapter Eleven

Angus had returned to bed eventually after finally mustering the strength to appear in the family room, but at least had been coaxed into having a shower under his own steam and don a fresh pair of pyjamas. More encouragingly, he had taken a pictorial book of Rhodesian wildlife with him, which he absently-minded scanned as he alternatively scratched Tom, then Dog's, heads.

Elizabeth and Kate sat before the fire in companionable silence. Eventually Elizabeth stirred and turned to Kate. "You may well tell me to mind my own business, but before this dreadful affair it seemed to everyone you and Angus were very close," she said. "Now I just see your professional nurse's face when you look at my son."

Kate paled slightly. It was on the tip of her tongue, which she knew had become increasingly acidic over the past months, to tell Elizabeth to mind her own bloody business. But then she remembered the many small acts of kindness Angus' mother was always performing – the cake which had arrived at the hospital on Kate's birthday when Angus was away, the approval on how Kate had redecorated Angus' bachelor apartment.

She sighed. "It's been coming for months now," she began. "I never knew when he was going, when he was coming back. And it seemed every time he came back he was a little more distant. I, both of us, had to reach harder and harder to reach the beautiful Angus inside...the man I fell so in love with. I think I first noticed it with his eyes. They no longer sparkled but seemed fixed in the distance. His mouth would smile, but the eyes remained cold and distant.

"Then we seemed to slowly lose our passion for each other." Elizabeth was woman of the world enough to know what *that* meant. She herself still yearned for Jonathon's touch after all these years.

"I thought we were becoming more like siblings than lovers... but then he started having nightmares. Tossing, turning, moaning in his sleep. And the worse it became the more he drank."

She paused. "Then there was the night he almost killed Nigel at the club. Nigel is a prat, but a harmless one. He was pretty drunk himself and goaded Angus with a baby-killer joke. The rest of the club had fallen deathly silent as Nigel's manners, but I will never forget the way Angus erupted from our booth and smashed Nigel throughout the bar. It took five men to drag Angus off him.

"When he came to his senses, he looked around at the destruction and at Nigel bleeding on the floor...and he cried. I took him home immediately, of course, but for the rest of the leave he was remote and barely grunted and hardly ate. Although he drank a bottle of gin a day."

Tears were by now coursing down both Kate and Elizabeth's faces. "That was the end of it for me...the beginning of the end had started long before."

So, Kate explained, she was on secondment in a last-ditch attempt to bring Angus back from the land of demons he occupied. She was in daily contact with Sally, who reported Daniel was in a very similar state, although attempting through his Matabele pride to disguise many of the symptoms. She also wondered how many of the Leopards had simply gone back to their villages and were not getting any help at all. That, Elizabeth, consoled her, had been one of Jonathon's top priorities on his return to Salisbury.

"I wonder," Elizabeth said, after a pause, "if you really know what Angus and Daniel and the boys did out in the bush? The polite military term is 'search and destroy' enemy strongholds, to pursue terrs through thick and thin and not rest until they were all accounted for. Then they had to gather the information the terrs had, discovering new targets and getting there before the enemy to head them off. Again – destroy."

Kate had heard rumours, but mainly from badly-wounded men in the hospital, many of them delirious and ranting. Now she focussed totally on Elizabeth and hardly noticed the topping up of brandy in her glass, which she saw with vague surprise was empty.

"They created killers out of our boys," Elizabeth relentlessly continued. "There were never any accounts of wounded. A suspected village would be infiltrated by men like Daniel, and once confirmed as a terr stronghold, would be obliterated. You may have heard of the Vietnamese village My Lai... a total slaughter. Rhodesia in the far bush is full of them. Not by the Leopards, they were far more selective, but by other units. But the Leopards came across their bloody handiwork time and again. And often the most merciful action was to put wounded survivors who had managed to hide from the massacre out of their misery. But having said that, and it was never reported, I'm sure the Leopards' blood lust overcame them on occasion. The occasional village just too tempting to be plucked, the innocent caught up with the guilty.

"Some of our men, perhaps some of the Leopards, are as guilty of war crimes as the terrorists.

"They created killers out of our boys," she repeated softly, staring now into the fire. "And Angus was their leader. One day, as long as there is a God, he would have had to account for it. Perhaps," she gestured to the bedroom wing, "That time has come."

Kate felt very small on the sofa, as if she had shrunken within herself. She'd heard the rumours of course: "Leopards got a major bag of floppies out near Mutely," had been one persistent tale on the ward. She knew who the Leopards were of course, secret force or not, but had no idea about floppies. It was only when she had mustered the courage to ask a recovering SAS sergeant the meaning that she found the dreadful truth.

The sergeant had looked at her with compassion, but ingrained honesty forced him to reply: "Floppies, Sister, are newly dead gooks. They flop around when they are hit by bullets." Kate had to remove herself from the ward to vomit until there was nothing left inside.

"So how many floppies did you bag this time out," she'd queried Angus on his eventual return from the bush. Angus had shot her a cruel, calculating look and refused to answer. He also pointedly retired to the guest room on their return to the apartment and she had heard faint murmurings as he talked quietly with Daniel on the phone. Kate cried herself to sleep that night.

"On the other hand," Elizabeth pointed out. "How many of our farmers have been killed by terrs, or ambushed on the roads. How many have had their workforce driven off their land – or just murdered? Angus told me once he estimated more than two thousands terrs roaming around his particular area and things are much, much worse further north around the Mount Darwin region. Our boys are doing their best, but it's like putting your finger in the leaking dyke."

She leaned towards Kate and continued: "We could have stopped all this fifteen, even ten years ago. Franchise Black landowners; create a Black middle class who had no desire for revolution and even less desire for communism. Black Africans are not communists, they at heart are capitalists. Some land, some say in the running of the country, some rights you and I take for granted. But we denied them and they turned to those who would gladly support an armed struggle – communists.

"We Whites made the same painful mistake as other African countries – Kenya, Uganda, Tanzania, and Zambia. We refused to create a viable Black middle class. We Whites wanted it all. Now, I fear, we will be left with nothing."

Kate was shocked. At the core of her beliefs had been the natural order of things, the eventual return to the status quo, and a return to peace.

"So are Angus and his men just wasting their time?" she asked a tremor in her voice.

"No," Elizabeth stated firmly. "Now we are committed to this dreadful course of action, however violent, we must stand firm.

Perhaps through that we may achieve a negotiated peace with room for us all. But if we cut and run – take the gap – we leave behind a country at the mercy of megalomaniacs like Mugabe. A truly evil man."

Kate reeled at the enormity of it and thought, not for the first time, of ignorance of her homeland. She had, after all, spent many years in South Africa. "Does Angus feel the same way," she asked.

"Those were Angus' words – word for word – and Jonathon's," Elizabeth replied softly.

"In that case," Kate said with new-found fire in her voice: "We'd better make that stupid bastard better."

"That stupid bastard" remained mainly in bed and around the confines of the house for the next week. He spoke little, hesitantly and ate reluctantly. But he ignored the alcohol, which Elizabeth and Kate saw as a good sign. One day he ventured as far as the stables and the orphanage. Many of the orphans had reached the stage where they could be released, but chose for feelings of security to stay near the familiar homestead. Tom and Dog padded slowly in his wake as if it were now their adopted duty to care for the man.

Angus walked to the railings where so often he had whistled up Nelson. He had no energy to whistle, but saw to his surprise Nelson come around the corner of the stable and come to him, the intelligent brown eyes searching into Angus's now-faded green ones. Angus fumbled in his pocket for a mango he'd picked for just such a chance meeting and Nelson gently took it from his hand, nibbling it with slow pleasure.

Something about Nelson reached deep inside him and he patted the horse's head with a long, loving stroke. As Elizabeth and Kate watched secretly from the stoep, Angus reached out his other hand and ruffled both Nelson's ears. Nelson responded by leaning closer to Angus with a slight wicker of content. Angus' attention slowly focussed totally on the horse and it seemed he lost some of his now-habitual slouch and stood straighter.

He seemed to make a private decision and disappeared into the stable, emerging with riding gear, the bridle and saddle. Going through the fence, he gently saddled Nelson and fitted the bridle and bit. There was none of the old games – like the knee into Nelson's gut to push out the wind the horse invariably sucked in when being saddled to allow a bit more room.

With obvious effort, Angus mounted. He swayed for a moment, and then grasped the pommel with one hand, the reins with the other.

"Oh, God no!" Elizabeth hissed. "He's too weak, he'll never control Nelson!" Kate waited a minute before replying. "Normally they would be at the other end of the paddock by now," she said. "They haven't moved an inch".

As if the pair heard them, Angus turned Nelson towards the wide expanse. Rather than bolt, Nelson ambled along at a pace just above walking speed, which he maintained as they disappeared behind the first outcropping kopje.

"Well," Kate said. "We may just have seen the first signs of rehabilitation. Let's see how hard he starts to push it now." To Elizabeth, she explained: "The first major hurdle is psychological. Once the patient begins to take in familiar surroundings, attempt physical exercise, it is a major step forward." She had said it coolly, dispassionately.

"That *patient* happens to be my son," Elizabeth flared at Kate, turning abruptly and going back inside the house, to her private room where even Jonathon hesitated to enter without first asking permission.

Kate blushed and sank into a nearby chair. She analysed her feelings for Angus yet again. Was there still love there yet? Then she had a sinking feeling. What guarantee was there Angus harboured any feelings for her? More than once, despite his illness, she had noticed him, in his moments of stability, regarding her with inscrutable eyes.

The first month had now passed. Physically Angus was starting to fill out again; there was less uncertainty in his movement although he was a far cry from Angus at his peak. Mentally he remained withdrawn although she had overheard occasional murmurings between the man and his mother.

Each day now Angus and Nelson rode off, gradually increasing the pace to a reasonable canter but nowhere near a full-blown gallop. But for reasons unfathomed he never went near the Pool.

"Have you noticed one thing?" Kate asked Elizabeth one morning. "Angus never takes his guns with him." Elizabeth replied in the affirmative. "They've stayed locked in the gun room ever since he came home," she said. "But out on the farm I've seen Angus and Nelson simply disappear – one moment they are riding with you, the next they're nowhere to be seen." It was a weak answer and she knew it.

Then one day Angus requested a "mighty" food basket from Matilda and set out at first light, warning he would not be back until dark, if then. He cantered in a different direction, to the east and again seemed taller in the saddle. Elizabeth had her suspicions, but kept quiet in front of Kate, who was once again in a slightly querulous mood. "He's my charge," she said. "I'm meant to know where he's going. What happens if Foster-Jones drops in for a progress report?"

"Angus is in charge of Angus," Elizabeth replied. "And the eminent professor is in Salisbury – a snippet she had learned over the phone the previous evening from Jonathon. Sure enough Angus re-appeared just before midnight, slightly the worse for Cape Brandy but for the first time with a small contented smile on his face.

"How is Daniel?" Elizabeth artlessly enquired. "'Bout the same as me," Angus replied. There were few secrets from his mother. "And Sally is a bloody tyrant. Makes Kate seem like Florence Nightingale." Kate, who was in the room, blushed and once again renewed her opinion of her "patient".

There were some men, she recalled, who through natural fitness of mind and body could bounce back far quicker than others – but then also, some of whom would never be the same again.

She looked closely, but surruptiously at Angus. He was almost standing his full height now, his hair had regained much of its natural gloss, and the beard he had chosen to grow was a coppery-gold which very much suited him. And, more importantly, he was increasingly joining in the conversation, although it was very much centred on the farm and its immediate needs. War, it seemed, was a taboo subject.

Angus poured a nightcap of cognac and sat before the fire. "We talked about further developing our experimental crops. And crossing more of HillView's bulls with Daniel's beasts. Sharing our labour forces more."

"But," he frowned and the elephant which had been in the room was finally heard.

"To do all that, we need to look at our security forces," he almost whispered.

Elizabeth ruffled Angus' hair, while Kate felt the hairs on the back of her neck rise. "Funnily enough, the Colonel is coming down for lunch tomorrow," she said. "He may have some ideas about that."

Chapter Twelve

The Colonel arrived with his driver in his personal car, in this case a gleaming blue BMW freshly buffed that morning. No dilapidated jeeps for the colonel, adding to which he had a rather painful case of piles caused, Angus sourly thought, from sitting on his arse too much.

But he bounded up the stairs to the stoep, where the remains of breakfast were being cleared and accepted a juice and coffee. He went out of his way to charm Elizabeth, who nonetheless looked at him like he was selling out-of date encyclopaedias and then soliticitly enquired after Angus' wounds.

The colonel looked at Elizabeth. "Perhaps, my dear, you don't want to hear all of this? He enquired. "Nonsense," Elizabeth retorted. "I've done more to put him back together than the army ever has."

The colonel accepted the implied rebuke on the chin. "Very well, then, I'll carry on." He visibly steeled himself. "You've made a remarkable recovery on all counts, from all accounts," he told Angus, who wished the man would stop pontificating and get to the point.

"But...you are simply not up to the Leopards any more. You've done too much at too much cost."

Angus reacted angrily. "What cost is too much for my country?" he asked sarcastically. "So I'm to be put on the shelf ... another man who couldn't pay the price?" Elizabeth touched his arm with empathy. "Let the colonel finish, dear," she said. Angus smelt a trap, something which had been cooked up behind his back, but brought his temper back to simmering point.

"You will still, if you choose, be a key advisor, perhaps our *key* advisor, on future Leopard operations, Angus. However, it is my view, and the view of the Brig, that you are too valuable to squander running around in the bush.

"But – we have another mission for you. The outlying farms are coming under increasingly violent terrorist attack. They are starting to rule the night and the horror of what they are doing to the farmers, wives and children are atrocities. To say nothing of their treatment of the Black labour. They are torturing them, driving them from their homes, kidnapping young teenagers for forced indoctrination into the gook cause."

Angus sat back, slightly mollified. It was, after all, touching on the subject he had discussed with Elizabeth the previous night.

"What we need is a training force for farm defence, to ensure that each farm has at least four men capable of mounting serious resistance. We've so far seen single farmwives drive off the gangs with nothing but rifle fire, but those times are rapidly changing. Of course, not all the attacks are carried out by Charlie Tangos. Some are just bands of bandits making the most of the situation to loot and kill. The terrs, are however, becoming more organised. Some farmers have already been forced from their lands, some have moved to nearby towns and are virtually absentee farmers. There are lands lying fallow for lack of attention. But most are determined to stick it through, hell or highwater."

That would required a hell of a lot of manpower, was Angus' first thought. There were thousands of farms, but not all in vulnerable positions and many farmers had instigated their own, adequate, security measures. But against the new wave of attacks, with mortars, rockets and rifles, they had vastly decreased resistance capabilities.

The farmers, by Government admission, had become the frontline of the war. Until relatively recently in the Melsetter district, near Umtali the number of farms that had previously been worked profitably, was forty five. Two years' later there just eight.

But despite the incredible hardships, Rhodesia, since sanctions were imposed by the free world, led by Britain and America, had doubled its agricultural production. However, local manpower to thwart the raids had thinned to the point that it was at snapping point. It was worse for the Black African farmers, who ran cattle and grew crops on an area larger than the total size of Britain. They were forbidden by the terrs, at pain of death, to dip their cattle against deadly disease, their villages forced to feed and protect the terrs during the daytime as they blended into village life – a classic Vietnam guerrilla tactic.

All this passed through Angus's mind as he studied the colonel's proposal from all angles.

"We need a hell of a lot of manpower," he voiced the thought aloud. The colonel nodded.

"Let me tell about one cock-up which illustrates why we need action and action now. One farmer from around here was dispatched to a farm north of Salisbury as their security man. When he got there, he found the farmer he was replacing was also on defensive duty – at the Bulawayo chap's own farm. With bullshit like that happening, this is a big job, for sure Angus, but done properly we can make a huge difference.

"Now, manpower," he continued. "We think four full-time security-trained men at each farm would act as a powerful deterrent. How many staff do you have in your quarters here?" he asked, seemingly off the top of his head.

"About a hundred," Angus replied. "Many are off with the military, of course. Not counting women and children, about forty."

"How long would it take you to find four reliable men and train them in the rudiments of security work?" the colonel asked. "We're not talking Leopard standards, or even army standards. Just good enough to do the job of guarding the homestead at night and the ability to shoot straight without panicking."

For weapons, he further clarified, FN FAL's would be issued, the standard weapon of the Rhodesian army. Any mention of Leopard-style specially-obtained M16s, or perhaps secret caches of AK47s, was left unsaid.

Angus found himself leaning forward as if to embrace some positive news after such a grim time at the fireface, which had reaped such a terrible cost. "We train five, not four," he planned. "The fifth will have military experience and knowledge and to him we give the task of training further men at other farms. That way we could mushroom in the quickest way. Almost every farm has men who have served and they won't have forgotten – or forgiven."

The colonel was impressed. What had started as a vague idea was fast becoming a reality. He had agreed with every aspect of Angus's impromptu plans and once again was reminded as to why the man seated opposite him in the sun on the stoep was one of Rhodesia's highest decorated soldiers. And had closed to within a devil's breath of paying the ultimate price. That prompted another thought and he silently cursed himself for the oversight.

"As I said, you remain a Leopard, or at least a Leopard top brass," he said, fishing into his lapel pocket. He handed the major's rank bars onto the table. "We can't have you running around in a senior post as a raggedy-arsed captain, now, can we?" More softly, he continued: "They were my own. I would be honoured to pass them to you."

Angus started, then looked from the gleaming bars to the colonel's eyes. He picked the bars up and held them in his hand. "I am deeply honoured, Sir," he sincerely said.

Elizabeth, who had remained so silent both men had forgotten her presence, suddenly clapped and kissed both Angus and then the colonel, who to his credit turned a beetroot red. "And now that is settled, a celebration! Champagne!" She rang the bell for Gideon.

"Perhaps just the one," the colonel demurred as he smiled wryly to Angus. "Now I have to go and convince Daniel."

Chapter Thirteen

Daniel, also almost fully recovered, had just one question of the colonel, once the scheme was explained to him. Daniel himself had recovered much of his ebony gloss and put back most of the significant weight he had lost. His wife, Csadsa, had taken Daniel under her wing like an angry lioness will protect her injured lion cub. Daniel, after almost two months was, to put it bluntly, feeling smothered.

"Is Angus in this business?" he said. Daniel would make no move without his blood-brother beside him.

"Angus is in and has dedicated forty men to the effort," the colonel replied. He had explained the training scheme, which to Daniel made perfect sense – and like Angus regarded it as long overdue. He had a similar number of men available, most of whom were veterans and had the military experience necessary to train up the security teams.

"Of course," Daniel told the colonel, "many of these vulnerable farms have vets of their own on the labour force. But time is against us, yet again. These poor bastards are fighting off the gooks while they try to avoid bankruptcy."

Daniel took a further huge draught of beer and refilled the colonel's gin glass with his own heavy hand. He looked out at his land, leased on the peppercorn rent from the Dunrows and with a healthy crop of maize starting to sprout.

"Let me give you a quotation from a book I was reading last night." The colonel almost blinked, but remembered a Dunrow scholarship had seen Daniel through the same schools as Angus and Daniel was, in fact, a highly-educated man. The colonel privately swore at his own ingrained prejudice.

"An English chap, called Lord Moran. He was Winston Churchill's personal physician for more than 25 years," Daniel began. "About the courage in the First World War he wrote: Courage is a moral quality. It is not chance gift of nature...it is a cold choice between two alternatives; the fixed resolve not to quit...courage is willpower...a man's courage is his capital and he is always spending, The call on the bank may be only be the daily drain of the frontline or it may be a sudden draft which threatens to close the account. His will is perhaps almost destroyed by intense shelling or by bloody battle, or it is gradually used up by monotony, by exposure ... by physical exhaustion, by a wrong attitude to danger, its casualties, the war, to death itself.""

The colonel stared at Daniel in amazement. You memorized that?" he said. "Those are the words which sum up this whole horrible, bloody, fucking mess."

Daniel shrugged. "I paraphrased some of it, but essentially what Lord Moran was saying sixty years ago holds so true now... and we had another world war and a couple of 'police actions' in Korea and Vietnam. What the hell have we learned? Another quote...this time from one of our men: 'We don't look back in anger or forward in fear, but around us in awareness'."

The colonel shrugged. "In WWII we learned fascism could be defeated, in Korea and Vietnam we learned nothing except how to create slaughterhouses to keep politicians happy. But here, we are holding onto our land – I won't say it's our birthright – but you know better than most how many Blacks want this place to remain Rhodesia, where they can prosper and thrive in a safe environment.

"The world makes the mistake of tarring us with the brush of South Africa. Apart from the lack of the franchise, which we all know was a major mistake, there's bugger-all apartheid here.

But it makes it easy for those imposing the sanctions to lump us in with our southern neighbours. I've seen the television coverage when overseas – sjambok-wielding South African police pictured on a story about Rhodesia."

The colonel himself was amazed by the intensity of the conversation, and as lunch came and went he and Daniel became more philosophical. Sure, he as the colonel and Angus had spoken many times, and crossed swords just as many, over the war, its motivations and implications, but he realised this was really the first really in-depth analysis he had shared with a Black man.

"This militia, for want of a better term, is seven years' overdue. But better late than never, I suppose," Daniel said.

He abruptly broke the mood. Perhaps he felt he had been too open with the colonel, who although was known and trusted by all his men, was still a senior officer. He and Angus had many such discussions, on the stoeps, in the bush, in the pubs. And perhaps the most angering aspect of it all lay in the answer: There was no answer. This war would pan out to a dreadful climax, one way or another.

"We'll start training our own men this week, should only take a few days, then sent them out to the other farms to recruit the others," Daniel said. I suggest we have a couple of flying forces, capable of quick movement to reinforce the guards. I also suggest we thoroughly vet all the labour compounds – there have been plenty of rumours of the gooks hiding among the labourers by day and attacking the farmhouses come night. The farmers themselves often chose to ignore this, like the colonialists in Kenya who insisted that Jomo the houseboy could not be Mau Mau, until he slit their throats with the carving knife he had just used on the roast beef. The farmers must individually identify each of the workers, sometimes in the compounds at night, because there have also been cases of the terrs hiding out there at night."

The colonel, who had been scribbling notes in a small pad, blinked: "You have proof of this?" he demanded.

"Absolutely," Daniel retorted. "And you should have the report on your desk. Tom Terry, leading cattleman, terrs tracked to his front gate then disappeared. Tom refused to believe any terrs could be hiding in the compound and the next night he and his sixteen year old son were murdered. His wife escaped only by hiding in the safe room."

The colonel's normally florid features flushed further. He knew of the report, but like so many others had seen little he could do post the event. Now, perhaps by becoming pro-active the tide could be held back, if not turned.

He rose, a bit unsteady from the gin and headed for his car, the door held open by his driver. "Anything you need, anything you want, you have it," he promised Daniel. "Get the job done."

Daniel drove to HillView the next day. The pair hadn't seen each other since Angus' ride over with the picnic hamper and both were privately pleased with the progress they saw in each other's health... there were obvious signs; fresh lines etched in their faces, their posture not quite as robust as before, occasional silences before sentences. Both looked older than their years and both radiated a quiet nervous energy which brought with it slight shakes of their hands as they toasted each other with Castle beer. The colonel was right, Daniel thought, neither were Leopard material anymore. Yet through their experiences they still had much to offer.

"We're not quite Dad's Army yet," Daniel quipped. Angus laughed, a rarity which saw Matilda poke her head from the kitchen in consternation, only to relax and allow herself a smile, and a personal pat on the back. The two boys, her favourite boys, together again as it should be.

Angus and Daniel leant closer together and quietly compared notes about their battle to rejoin the human race. They had markedly similar stories – the nightmares, the tremors, the sudden and irrational fears, the slowly coming to terms with their injuries. Both agreed the physical injuries had been a minor annoyance, but the giant mental hurdles had been absolute hell on earth. Neither held the slightest grudge over their enforced absence from each other. Each had dealt with the crisis in his own way.

"Before we talk business, and before lunch, I have an idea," Angus said. "Let's visit the Pool." Daniel was well aware through the infallible grapevine which existed between Matilda and the Nkumo's own head of household, Maria, that Angus had not been anywhere near the Pool in the past two months. He immediately agreed, but pointed out, with dignity, that his pinned knee precluded him from riding any horse in the notoriously invigorated Dunrow stables.

"Fine," Angus said cheerfully. We'll take the MG instead." Daniel blinked. Angus had always been car-mad, but an MG in the wilds of HillView? As if reading his friend's mind, Angus continued: "I got the chaps to knock out a bit of a track from here to the pool, with a few racing corners in it. Frikkie has beefed up the suspension and tickled the motor – you'll love it!"

And once the initial fear of approaching this-is-certain-death speed wore off, Daniel had to admit he did, in fact, love it. The howl of the wind, the roar of the juiced-up motor, the rock music blasting from the stereo tape system and the clouds of red dust behind them spelt nothing but carefree fun. For a moment, Daniel wondered when he had last had one of those carefree dashes into absolute enjoyment and immediately dismissed the thought. He simply couldn't remember. Angus drove as ever he did, fast, accurate, with total concentration – and a grin on his face like that of a teenager let lose in Dad's prized car.

Too soon, they pulled up in a cloud of red dust at the gates of the pool. As passenger, the honour fell to Daniel to creak the now-rusty gate open and jump, literally, back in the car as Angus belted the last two hundred metres to the Pool. With the motor turned off and quietly ticking as it cooled, both men quietly contemplated the scene.

"Not much has changed here," Angus said, almost sadly. "This place will last forever." He and Daniel unloaded the wicker baskets and spread a large picnic rug on the native grass. "We're getting soft, old man," he teased. "Perhaps we should recommend these blankets to the Leopards as our first act as advisors."

Daniel tensed. This was possibly the ideal opening. "About that," he started. "Advisors to the Leopards..."

"Pure and absolute charity by the colonel," Angus agreed. "Maybe the odd special job here and there, but I've no wish to be a desk warrior. No, this new assignment makes much sense to me. Train those most in need."

And as they devoured the cold chicken and beef, with Matilda's homemade bread, washed down with Castle cooled in the Pool they fell to animated discussion. Angus had brought large-scale maps of the areas of interest and they straight away identified the major farming operations at greater risk.

The afternoon hours melted away as they argued contingencies back and forth, but each was reaching for a common goal and both realised it was common sense which would help achieve those goals.

Angus eventually stood and stretched, then disrobed and plunged naked into the cool green waters of the Pool. Daniel was a step behind him. They both floated as they made peace with themselves and soaked in the therapeutic soothing of the Pool. "Do you know," Angus said. "The last time I was here was a long, long time ago...with Kate."

Angus had not mentioned Kate to Daniel at all since their meeting that morning and Daniel, respecting Angus' silence, had made no comment. He thought about it now, but still decided to let Angus make the running on that topic, if he so wished.

However, it seemed the subject was closed, as Angus swam to the bank and roughly dried himself with the blanket, scrupulously leaving half of it dry for Daniel and then dressing again.

Daniel followed suit and they motored at a far more sedate pace back to HillView in the gathering darkness. That Daniel would stay the night was without question and after a gargantuam dinner from Matilda's kitchen, shared by Elizabeth who was delighted to see Daniel again and a very quiet Kate, they pulled out the maps again, with large sheets of plain paper to continue the planning. Elizabeth and Kate both retired from the room for coffee in the sitting room.

It was then that Kate re-entered the room, which was fast taking on the appearance of a military planning centre. She stood silently for a moment before Angus glanced up and immediately stopped what he was doing.

"Kate!" he smiled. There was no return smile and Angus felt a shiver of trepidation in his bones.

"I've come to say goodbye," Kate barely whispered, "My assignment was for two months to get you back on your feet and you are well and truly very advanced along that path." The speech sounded rehearsed to Angus, but he said nothing. "The two months is almost up and you are ready to take your life back into your own hands. Daniel, Sally will say the same to you when you go home. Our mission here is over...your new one is just beginning."

Angus sat stunned for a moment, but he recognised the truth behind the words. Besides, it seemed he and Kate had only communicated about basically medical matters and very little else. Still, he felt a sick, sliding sensation in his gut. As he had recovered, so had his perception and he realised, belatedly it now seemed, the deep underlying courage Kate had mustered to nurse him back to health. The fact he would no longer be doing the dirty work, the guts-or-glory stamp of the Leopards made little difference to Kate. Yes, he would be returning to the bush, yes there would be violence, but this time it would be defensive, not offensive.

He masked his feelings with every piece of mental courage he could muster and rose to go to Kate. "Kate," he began and then choked. He kissed her chastely on the cheek. "You deserve a medal for everything you have done. Not just for me, but for Elizabeth as well. We would not have got through this had it not been for you. Thanking you is terribly inadequate, but it is from the bottom of my heart."

Kate gave him an inscrutable look, then turned and left the room. Had Angus been able to see through walls, he would have seen the tears pouring down her face. Damn you, Angus Dunrow, damn you and your kind, even Daniel, to hell. She hardly felt Elizabeth put her arms around her in comfort and draw her tear-stained face to her shoulder.

"Men," Elizabeth said. "Can be complete and utter bastards."

Chapter Fourteen

It had taken Daniel and Angus less than three days to whip their eighty-strong forces into shape. Many had recent war experience, even more had friends and family both on the white-owned farms and their black contempories.

"We'll send two men into each farm to train up the rangers," Angus suggested to Daniel. "If all goes well, two weeks training should do it – how to recognise landmines, how to protect the farmhouses and how to sniff out terrs infiltrating the labour force. One will stay with the trainees, giving us a stick of five on each farm."

Daniel considered for a moment and agreed. "That's forty farms to start with. I suggest we stick to our plans and target the Umlimo region first – with strong emphasis on the Black farmers. Six and a half thousand have been slaughtered so far. We know the tortures they have endured. A quarter of a million of their cattle have been killed or stolen this year. The poor bastards have no protection."

"As for the white areas," and Daniel reeled off a list of vulnerable townships. Umlimo itself had been mortared five times, but other outlying outposts - Melsetter and Cashel, Chipinga, Concession and Inyanga to name a few were under almost unbearable pressure despite a heavy presence of troops, whose main task was to reinforce the more populated areas. "The poor bloody farmers are relying on pop guns and radios to protect themselves."

Arms, ammunition and other protective devices, including fences, phosphorus flares and spotlights, sensor wires outside the wired parameters were astronomical in cost. But they were gladly funded by bodies including the Government, industry, the military itself and volunteer donors from the larger cities. Annually, it would cost millions of dollars, but still a pittance in relation to the value of agricultural output from viable farms.

The men were detached that day, except for the flying squad of ten men, led by Angus and Daniel, who would carry out spot checks on the progress and respond as quickly as possible to immediate threats. To overcome the danger of landmines being laid on the access roads (a routine procedure), Angus had wheedled a helicopter from Rhodesia's dwindling forces. It was kept in a constant state of readiness at a forward base.

Within days, by radio, the reports began to drift in. Particularly in the black areas, the ranger initiatives were met with open arms. In many of the black farms, the rangers had trained not four, but up to ten men to be the vigilantes. All had been thoroughly vetted and many had previous combat experience. It was an initiative Angus welcomed. He personally supervised the distribution of weapons to the volunteers and only when he was satisfied they were in a state of readiness did he release the rangers to move to other villages.

Just one white farmer was proving reluctant. James Potter had always been a rugged individualist, determined to run his farm his way. He cared for his labour force as he cared for his prize cattle and there, Angus thought, laid the groundwork of the problem. James did not value the return he could potentially get from listening to the wisdom and the vital intelligence from his Black workers. Angus decided he would take the matter into his own hands and arrived just before noon by his reinforced LandRover at the Potter farm. Perhaps it was another measure of the man, but the landholding, since his grandfather's time, had always been called Potter's Farm.

He immediately saw it was well defended externally with heavy chain-link fences around the house's property, defensive one and a half metre high brick walls built nearer the house, trees cleared to deny stealthy approach to the house should the fence be breached. Three huge Doberman dogs were now tethered in the shade of a gazebo, to be set loose near nightfall.

Angus's rangers sat forlornly in the shade afforded at the side of their jeep. He grinned at them and waved, then made his way to the front door, protected as were all the windows by steel grenade shields.

Potter himself was sitting on a lounge near the door and was watching Angus approach. He made no effort to rise. "What the fuck do you want, Dunrow?" was the less-than-courteous greeting.

Angus studied him. He was a bull of a man, with an aggressive slant to his shoulders and head. He decided the blunt approach would be the best. There was no pussy-footing with *this* bloke. "To try and talk some fucking sense into that melon you mistakenly think contains a brain," he said. "I'm sure you're alright, Jimmie boy, tucked away in your fortress and bugger the rest of the world, including your workforce – who for some fucking unbelievable reason are still here and haven't pissed off for more secure parts."

Potter blinked in surprise and reared up from the longue, then thought better of it. Angus topped him by six inches and by many notches in physical ability. "So what am I fucking supposed to do," he acidly enquired. "Nursemaid them?"

"How many do you know by name," Angus shot back. "You've about sixty male labourers here, how many would you recognise in the street?"

Potter was slightly taken aback. "Most of them probably," he began, and then trailed off under the unflinching green eyes boring into his. "Well, some of them. I don't exactly invite them to the club for lunch!" The miserable attempt at humour fell flat.

"Let's take a walk," Angus suggested. "Just say hello by name to the ones you know." Reluctantly, Potter accompanied Angus, hurrying to match the big man's long-legged stride.

"You've got bugger all working in the field just there," Angus pointed. "I know grain's hard to get, so there's not much need for labour, apart from weeding, so let's start there."

Potter reluctantly agreed. In truth, he knew most by sight, but there were many he regarded as just fitting into the background, like the maize itself, or his cattle. He greeted the first man with confidence: "Hello there Innocent!" he boomed, clapping the man on the back and moving to the next man. Angus lingered.

"Is your name Innocent?" he enquired softly. "No, Mambo," the man replied. "My name is Mezzo". Question asked and answered, Angus thought and hurried to catch up with Potter. "Let's go to the compound," he said. "Don't greet them by name, just point out the ones who you recognise. More to the point, point out the ones you don't"

Potter puzzled over the request, but obediently entered the nearby compound, where about forty men were resting in the shade while their womenfolk prepared meagre lunches. The main meal always was taken in the evening.

Looking around, Potter almost visibly sighed with relief. "Him I know...and him...and...Him...and him...." The list went on for a while until Angus cut it short. "Now the ones you don't. Think very carefully about this." He fought down the impulse to say a decline in recognition could mean a death sentence.

"Well, now, some of these younger blokes I don't recall seeing before," he said. "But then I usually let the headman choose his labour."

Angus called over the headman, who he could see was badly frightened. Headmen usually got the chop first if they didn't co-operate with terrorist demands. "Who are the five sitting in the shade behind you," he asked quietly in IsiNdebele. "Don't look at them, don't point. Just tell me who they are...their names."

The headman quaked. "They arrived yesterday," he mumbled, "They demanded food, shelter and women." Angus nodded for the man to continue. Rape was usually a prime prerequisite. "I do not know their names, they called each other comrade, one is Comrade China, and another Comrade Butcher...I do not know the rest."

Angus thanked him with the deep courtesy reserved for elders and told him to return to his people. If asked by the comrades he was simply to say the white men were checking health and ration levels. He motioned Potter, who had stood by in stunned silence to leave the compound. "Now do you see your problem," he rhetorically asked. "Five terrs nicely at home in your compound. Maybe tonight they strike and you have no labour forces left." Potter nodded dumbly, shocked to the core. Another of his precious beliefs had been shattered.

"Now we are going to do it my way," Angus said and whistled to the rangers, who rose as one and cocked their weapons. "We go in fast, in the Rover and those five gentlemen sitting in the shade over there cease to exist," he ordered. One of the rangers had been SAS in a former life and grinned mirthlessly. "Fish in a barrel," he said. Angus cautioned him the terrs would almost certainly have Ark's nestled behind them.

"And for Christ's sake, just those five," he emphasised. "Anybody else running is just trying to get out of the way."

They idled the Rover to within 10 metres of the compound gate, casually looking around as if on another boring recon. Then Angus gunned the motor and swung through the gate, straight at the five gooks. He broadsided the vehicle, but the rangers were already firing their FNs. Angus joined in with his M16 but by then the job was almost done. The five terrs lay twitching on the ground, blood pouring from multiple wounds. One man had been neatly decapitated and blood fountained from his neck. The rest were in grotesque postures. Another had lost his arm, one had his eye hanging down to his mouth and another had been gut-to-chest shot. The final terr was the most gruesome. He had caught almost a full magazine from Angus and what little remained of him was barely recognisable as having once been human, just ten seconds earlier.

Angus and the rangers climbed down from the Rover and kicked the bodies apart. Sure enough, behind each lay an AK47 and one man had been carrying a satchel of Soviet-supplied grenades. Angus turned to Potter, who had wheezed his way into the compound and was now a deathly shade of pale. "Lesson learnt, James?" he politely enquired. Potter's response was to violently vomit.

Chapter Fifteen

After that, there was no possibility of arrogance or defiance from James Potter. He readily agreed to have a stick of rangers on his land and, Angus later heard, had not only helped select the most likely trainees but was also taking huge strides in getting to know his workforce. Additionally, he had a purpose-build clinic constructed near the compound and employed a female staff member with nursing experience to run it.

The next farm on his list to visit was temporarily run by one of the real old-time characters of Rhodesia. George Style was 75 years old and owned a large prosperous farm, with a hunting concession, just out of Salisbury, run with the help of his sons. Earlier on, George had volunteered for the police but been rejected on account of his age.

"Bastards," he had once told Jonathon Dunrow. "Half the pricks on the selection panel wouldn't know one end of a gun from the other". George had gone home and ruminated about the situation and come up with what he regarded as a brilliant solution – he would baby-sit farms in the dangerous regions while their owners took much-needed breaks. After a few stints, where battle-weary farmers, their wives and children had returned home refreshed after a stress-free month in South Africa, or at the coast in Mozambique before that border was permanently closed, George found himself almost fully-booked, often up to a year ahead.

George was also unique in that he didn't charge a cent. He also supplied most of his own food and drink. "I wouldn't want people to think I was out for a free ride," he'd told Jonathon. "These poor bastards – one of George's favourite descriptions – can't have a break, they're so worn down it's as much as they can do to pack the car and leave for a while."

That George was a loner, except for a small white dog which accompanied him everywhere, was self-evident. But occasionally on the farms, if the cook met his standards, he would hold long luncheons for neighbouring farmers, most of whom he had helped in the past.

And despite his own miniature dog, which was just a pet, George always had two pieces of advice for the border farmers– dog up, not down. German shepherds, Labradors, Ridgebacks, anything which had a loud bark and an aggressive attitude. "Seen the terrs run from dogs," he quoted. "And keep your guns with you all the time. They're no bloody good locked in a cupboard during the day."

He was a crusty character, of that there was no doubt and Angus, having heard so much from Jonathon about the man who had played guardian angel for more than 20 years had been eagerly looking forward to meeting him. George was currently installed at Mount Vista, a high-risk farm near Penhalonga, high in the Eastern Districts.

Angus had left the rest of the Flying Squad behind to continue moving from farm to farm, with plans to meet them later. He'd floored the accelerator to the floor on several parts of the road which could well have been ambush-prone and the huge motor in the Rover had relished the workout. So with the tell-tale trial of red dust billowing behind, he pulled into Mount Vista's homestead.

George himself came bustling out of the house. That he resembled a tough old rooster was Angus' first thought. Then he noticed from the way the man carried himself he was as tough as aged biltong. The handshake was crushing and the blue eyes twinkling from under the wrinkles of age.

"Hey man...they send you to check up on the old fella...make sure he's not eating too much of their beef?" was his initial enquiry, followed by a scatter-gun of other questions and comments about weather and cattle before he paused for breath.

"Angus Dunrow," Angus finally had the chance to intervene. He had been warned that George enjoyed a chat, the lengthier the better and replies were often optional. But he had also been alerted that George would seldom talk about himself.

"Dunrow..." George puzzled over it. "Angus Dunrow...". His furrowed brow cleared. "Ah yes, Jon's brat, the war hero." He glanced over Angus's uniform, which betrayed no signs of insignia or rank. "You've been in the wars," he observed the slight hunch Angus still carried and the lines on the young man's face. "Come in, come in...it's time for a tipple. At my age it's what keeps me going – good advice young man Make sure you take it."

Angus had already taken a liking to the man. His blunt manner, the sense of humour and, above all he remembered, the courage and compassion George had shown quite off his own bat made for a memorable character.

George's "tipple" was enough to make Angus gasp at the first mouthful. George noticed and grinned, displaying a full set of healthy teeth. "Pickles you," he said. "Christ, the number of blokes my age pushing up daisies in Salisbury Cemetery because they wouldn't get off their arses and do something with their lives... buggered by the time they were seventy!"

"You know, the secret to getting older is not to get older". In the abrupt manner of change in subject matter to which Angus was becoming accustomed, he said, the twinkling eyes fixed on Angus' own," What brings you here?"

Angus managed another sip of the rocket-fuel and gave George his full attention as he outlined the plans for the sticks of permanent rangers to be stationed at the vulnerable farms. "This is defensive, not offensive," he said. "There are plenty of blokes chasing the terrs around in the bush, but the majority of farms have bugger all – he was slipping into George's vocabulary involuntarily - and it's time that was addressed."

111

George grunted. "Several years too bloody late, but better now than never," he conceded. "Mind you, you could be doing me out of a job," he chuckled. "But I suppose they'll always need a boss man around – there are plenty of really good foremen in the labour force, but do you know just about none of them can drive? I have to take the bloody truck into town to get supplies."

Angus thought of what that simple statement entailed and marvelled at it. George, seventy-five, driving a truck along ambush-prone and land-mined roads alone, except for a bodyguard or two, and passing it off as if it was a casual meander into the local church on a Sunday. His respect grew.

George pondered for a bit. "Those blokes charging around the bush hunting the terrs," he thought out loud. "Ah yes...that's it. You were the leader of that outfit called the Leopards, weren't you?" Angus blinked. The Leopards were a closely-guarded secret, supposedly. "Don't worry," George chuckled. "Jon talked about it a bit in Salisbury after a couple of my tipples."

Angus was surprised that after a couple of tipples Jon hadn't let George in on the entire war strategy. The man had a way of drawing information and obviously possessed a cracker of a memory. "Yes," he said, stretching his still-stiff back. "We paid the price, though."

George was suddenly serious, another of his mercurial mood swings. "Paying the price, paying the piper...how many of the cream of our Rhodesian crop have done that?" he mused, mixing metaphors. "Too fucking many." He fixed Angus with a piercing look. "Good luck young man. But I have a feeling you won't be too defensive for too long. The terrs are getting bolder. Caught a few of the bastards threatening my chaps in the fields a week ago. The feed will be good in that patch for the new season – nothing like some blood-and-bone to liven up the soil."

"Where do you go next? Angus enquired. George, it seemed, would take a break himself with his long-suffering wife in Salisbury then head for another hot-spot to allow another family a well-earned break.

"The real reason I came, actually," Angus confessed, "was that I had heard so much about you and wanted to meet you – really, simply so I could say I had. And it's been an absolute pleasure and privilege."

George chuckled. "At least you're honest, take after your father that way, I suppose. But don't let all the bullshit cloud your judgment, sonny. You have a power of work to do. Now," he checked his watch, it's lunch time".

Several hours later Angus weaved the Rover back to his rangers. The tipple had been followed by fine wine, specially brought in by George "to ward off the chilly nights" and later topped off with cognac. George himself had showed no ill-effects and chatted freely about a wide-ranging subject of topics: About crops and cricket, cattle and the castration of terrs, censorship of news, which was becoming draconian and Rhodesia's prospects at the negotiating tables at Lancaster House in London. But not once had he talked about himself and Angus realised George was essentially a very private man.

And a generous one. As Angus took his leave, somehow negotiating his way into the driver's seat, George had placed a carton of the luncheon wine in the back of the Rover. "Noticed you enjoyed it," he shrugged off Angus's effusive thanks.

His final words had been in Latin: Nili illegitimi carborundum. "Which means," as he noticed Angus' puzzlement: "Don't let the bastards grind you down!" Angus was still chuckling as he drove, one eye shut in an effort to steer in a straight line.

Then he thought again of a sobering statistic that George had casually thrown into the conversation. Zambia, to the north, once Northern Rhodesia, had world-class copper mines, but with the ascent of Kenneth Kaunda to power in the early 1970s, the mines had been nationalised and production had plummeted, almost overnight robbing that country of its major foreign exchange earnings, just as world prices were soaring. Grain once freely flowed across the border from Rhodesia, a practice which had been immediately stamped out, with Zambia choosing instead to buy its maize from Australia – at four times the price of the

Rhodesian produce. Zambia, once one of the most flourishing economies in Southern Africa, was now an economic and social basket-case.

Malawi, to the east, had taken a totally different tack. Also once part of the doomed Central African Federation, it had under President Kamuza Banda, introduced a government policy of almost total non-interference in the agricultural sector, to the point where the industry's tea, coffee and tobacco production was exported world-wide. It was also self-sufficient in food, and while disagreeing with Rhodesia's racial politics, had encouraged many displaced white farmers to re-settle and begin new operations in Malawi.

It was quite a remarkable parable, Angus thought, as he now found his other eye was focusing as well and the road had lost many of its twists and turns. He motored into Chongwe farm, where the rangers had moved in his absence and learned that once again the ranger policy was been warmly greeted.

Daniel greeted him with a cold beer. Angus groaned, but accepted the drink. "So how was the old bugger?" he asked. "Get you pissed on his tipples?" Angus gingerly nodded his head. He longed for aspirin but the beer was having a restorative effect.

A thought occurred to him: "You've met the old sod?" he asked Daniel. Daniel grinned and agreed. "About five years ago, we were on a bit of a safari around Beatrice and he was looking after a farm there. The Nkosi is a man."

Angus pondered the saying. Yes, George was a man, one of the highest compliments from the Matabele. He himself would have little problem calling the old fellow Nkosi.

Chapter Sixteen

So far it seemed the ranger concept had proved itself. There had been a small number of attacks, easily repulsed by the guard force and seemingly catching the terrs by surprise. Expecting an easy night out attacking farmhouses and labour compounds, they had run into spirited and hostile receptions and bolted, leaving several of their members sprawled dead on the fields.

And as per the policy, the guards did not pursue the retreating terrs except to determine the line of their retreat, which was instantly radioed to base, which promptly despatched any hunting units in the region to the last known vicinity. Once tracks, and often more than one bloodied trail were located, they were followed. Tracking at night was virtually impossible, but at first light the hunt would resume, often across the borders to more substantial terrorist encampments...and Angus and Daniel were particularly please to hear, sometimes by Leopards.

Sometimes the airforce were called in to bomb and napalm the bases, but more often it was the men of the army who carried out wholesale destruction.

The figures were speaking for themselves, Angus mused as he studied the first two months returns from the units. One guard had been lightly wounded, it was estimated up to two hundred terrs had paid the ultimate price. And, more importantly, agricultural production was on the rise again and once-abandoned farms were being re-occupied.

Angus had learned his lesson with the Leopards and insisted that no man remain in the field for more than four weeks, overlapping leave so the rangers were always bolstered by experienced men on the various farms. No ranger went in cold, extensive briefings were held. The farmers themselves had also rallied in other, more fundamental areas. There were no cold rations for the guards. "If the bastard gooks can run off hundreds of my cattle, I can always spare a few so these men eat beef!" had been James Potter's view, roundly adopted by the other settlers. Lunchtime braais and beer were common, but always ended early afternoon – there was no room for fat bellies and booze at night.

Two months, Angus mused. Six months would really tell the story, but the portents were healthy. Which brought him to a bout of introspection. It had been five months since he himself had taken a break. In that time his body had completely healed and the nightmares were long gone. The lesson learned from the Leopard days, he insisted none of his men stayed in the field for more than three weeks before going home for rest and recreation. But he had stayed at the headquarters, apart from regular inspection sorties out to the farms. He shook his head. What was good for the goose was good for the gander. But leave meant Salisbury. Salisbury meant Kate.

Should she still be there, he wryly thought. There had been no communication for five months and she could well have washed her hands of the country and headed south again. Angus realised he was procrastinating. Two weeks' leave would answer a lot of questions: Did she still think him a cold-blooded murderer, a member of the bloody elite which left a trail of slaughter behind them?

He left at first light the next day, firing up the Rover and driving at ambush-busting speed, burning the miles over both the bush tracks and finally the asphalt roads. It was a long drive, five hundred miles and Angus' mouth watered as he passed the Colonial Inn in Mbelo. But he resolutely sped on and within half an hour was pulling into the apartment's garage.

Joshua greeted him with genuine delight, with the special African hand shake that denoted respect. "Nkosi," he beamed. "You are here! But," he features fell for an instant, "there is little beer in the icebox and not much food. I go shopping immediately" and pulling a hessian shopping bag from behind the cupboard door he disappeared.

Angus, who had not managed to get a word in apart from the initial greeting, smiled in bemusement. The more things change, the more they can stay the same, he thought as he dumped his luggage on the floor and went into the kitchen to investigate the 'fridge. The "little" beer supply was a dozen ice-cold Castle lagers and Angus had knocked the top of one and drained half of it in one swallow. It had, after all, been a thirsty trip.

He showered the red dust off under alternatively hot-cold water and shaved, dressed casually and slumped into an easy chair in the living room. First things first, he thought. This could not be put off forever.

He rang the hospital and inquired whether Sister Kate Hansen was on duty that day. He thought, or probably imagined a slight pause of reluctance, but buoyed his spirits by the knowledge he had been in town for less than half an hour. Even the Bulawayo Bulletin, the affectionate name for the wives peering through windows with a phone in their hands, was not *that* efficient.

"Sister Kate *is* on duty, but cannot be disturbed," he was informed "Who shall I say called, please," the pleasant African voice came back on the line.

"No message, thank you very much," Angus courteously thanked the woman. So that was the first hurdle cleared. Opening another beer, he began to plot his campaign with almost military diligence.

After all, their last experience with Kate nursing Angus back to something approaching a human being had been a very trying time for both of them. Kate had been strictly businesslike then in her approach to his health, understanding of his wild mood swings, but there had been a distinct iceberg coolness between them.

Angus sunk further into the chair and came close to damning himself for a fool. Three months when he could barely string two words together, five months in the bush with no contact with her. Eight long, long months. In all probability she had been snapped up by one of the glamorous young doctors and was even now, perhaps even by now, engaged to marry.

Or she may have finally been totally sickened by the massive trauma cases which with she dealt with on a daily basis and the sight of Angus could prove a breaking point. Once again, Angus told himself, he was procrastinating,

It was time for action, man, he firmly laid down the rules for himself. He pondered some more: Flowers? He mentally kicked himself. Most of the wounded sent flowers to nurses and the hospital in general on their release. Flowers to a hospital...come on, he told himself...you can do better than that!

A formal invitation to dinner somewhere exclusive? He was jumping ahead of himself. She'd possibility laugh, show it to her new, supposed, lover before tossing it in the bin. Christ. Angus wracked his brain. He'd planned enough campaigns, but one to capture back a heart? He was a child in the woods...inspiration was what he needed. His army mates were no good, there would be plenty of ribald suggestions, but that was that. Previous girlfriends? Hell no...most of them would relish the Great Man brought down by a woman. Fuck it, Angus eventually thought. He was in the city to see her and see her he would. The worst scenario would be a curt and to the blunt point dismissal. He could hardly expect her to collapse in his arms in gratitude.

Man up, Angus told himself. He was carrying on like Matilda. Matilda! Now *there* was a thought. What would Matilda's reaction be. She would laugh until she cried, he decided, and almost instantly a possible answer came to him. Humour. It had worked in the early days with Kate...

He glanced at his watch. One-thirty in the afternoon. She finished at three. How the hell could he organise dancing elephants and cavorting ostriches in that time? Then he thought again. A traditional approach...an African traditional approach. Grabbing the phone he called every Matabele he knew in Bulawayo and within an hour had rounded up two dozen who still possessed their tribal skins of clothing, their spears and knobkerries. He also managed half a dozen women, whose job would be to ululate Angus' praises.

Within an hour he had them assembled in the park near the hospital, but well out of view. The Matabele warriors were fine sights, in their traditional garb and the women resplendent in their full-flowing costumes.

There was one major surprise. Daniel led the group. "What the hell are you doing here?" Angus blurted. "I was in town and heard what you had planned," Daniel chuckled richly. "This is just too damn good to miss."

"Fuck you, Daniel," Angus grinned without rancour and suddenly laughed itself. "If this doesn't work I'll take up celibacy. That in itself, prompted another belly laugh and because they had been speaking Sindabele, the rest of the group had understood and joined in with the riotous glee so much the trademark of the fun-loving Black Africans.

"Now," Angus quizzed Daniel. "You know what to do?" Daniel smiled in the affirmative and at just before three o'clock they moved to the section of the park directly opposite the hospital entrance.

The gathering of tradionally-clad Matabele warriors, armed with their spears drew some fearful glances from passers-by, but concerns were quickly diminished by the obvious joviality of the occasion.

Angus himself was isolated and hidden from view at the rear of the group..

At just after three the performance began, with the beautifully-haunting African voices lifting harmoniously into a tribal praise song, complemented by the higher pitch of the African women.

Many people grew to watch, until quite a crowd had gathered. There was no celebration due they knew of, but such was the overwhelming sense of occasion they remained transfixed.

Kate came out of the entrance. Angus was once again struck by her poise and beauty, which even after a horrendous shift in the emergency department remained with her, so she almost seemed to walk alone.

She too stopped. And immediately, so did the African song and dancing, with a loud thud of heels on the park grass. Led by Daniel, they approached her, until it was obvious she was being singled out. Kate showed no consternation, but rather smiled at Daniel, who she knew well as Sally's big brother.

Daniel detached himself from the group and came to her. "We wish you glorious tidings," he began, before launching into praise for her beauty and character.

"Daniel," Kate giggled; "What on earth is this and what do you want?"

Daniel shuffled his feet before her and finally spoke. "I come on a mission to present the cause of a brother, whose heart is sorely broken and can find no way to live without the enjoyment of basking in the sunshine of your glow," he began.

"This man is a warrior, but in matters such as these he is little better than a suckling child," he conceded. "It is for this we have gathered," and he indicated the traditional group behind him, "so we may help present his case. As his brother, I personally vouch for his honour and bravery. I also think he would raise many sons," he ventured.

They had spoken in Sindabele, as befitted the serious nature of the mission, but now Kate broke into English. "You have no brother for me," she accused, then stopped as if shot. "Except one ... a white man." Daniel nodded in solemn acknowledgement.

"Where is he?" she demanded. The ranks of the Matabele opened and from the rear Angus approached her, eyes fixed on hers. He'd lost weight, she irrelevantly noted, then saw the sparkle back in the green eyes and the erect carriage with which he strode.

Daniel retired a tactful distance, back to the group, but still within earshot. There was no way he would miss this, a meeting which would be the conversational fodder around many campfires for a long time ahead.

Kate stared at Angus until he came within touching distance. Then she reared back and slapped him with all her strength across the face. Angus' head reeled, but he did not move an inch. Nor did he rub the burning flash on his face. And he continued to gaze into her eyes. There was a collective sigh from the Matabele women. Many had longed to do just that to their own wayward warriors.

"You bastard, Dunrow," Kate hissed. "You complete and utter bastard."

"What the living *fuck* do you think you are on about?" Then suddenly she was in his arms, weeping. "You bastard," she repeated, though with a total lack of venom. "Couldn't you have just sent flowers?" The incongruity of the statement made Angus chortle, then laugh out loud. She had forgotten the deep, rich timbre of his laughter and this time she looked into his eyes and began to giggle in sympathy. "Only you, Angus...only you could have dreamt this one up."

The Matabele launched into a riotous song of joy and praise, the men and women both dancing to their music. The crowd of onlookers, many of whom were close friends of Kate and knew of Angus, roared with approval. Angus swept Kate into his arms again and lifted her to his head height, delivering a kiss which promoted further song and shouts of appreciation.

Kate blushed and mock-curtsied to the crowd. She momentarily left Angus' side and went to Daniel. With a total lack of reserve she hugged him and kissed him on the cheek, whispering in his ear: "Thank you, Daniel dear, thank you."

Angus took her by the arm and led her to Jonathon's BMW. He must remember to get the Jaguar back from the farm, he distantly thought.

Joshua had been aware of the plan from its inception. He'd heard the arranging phone calls and had already been filled in on the results by the black version of the Bulawayo Bulletin, often a far speedier and more accurate source than the white version.

The apartment was spotless, flowers were everywhere. A small coffee table stood at the side of the sofa, with Moet Chandon chilled in an ice bucket and two Waterford crystal champagne flutes. There was even gentle, romantic African music flowing from the sound system. Of Joshua himself, there was no sign.

They settled on the sofa, arms entwined and sipped the champagne, both savouring the moment. It was suddenly shattered by the ring of the telephone. Angus was about to ignore it, but it became too insistent an interruption and only very few, select, people had the number. He picked up the receiver and grunted a response, then looked at Kate in surprise.

"It's for you," he said, giving her the handpiece. Kate looked stunned and listened to an obviously female voice on the other end. "Yes," she eventually managed. "Thank you so much." She hung up and looked to Angus in disbelief. "That was Matron," she said. Angus groaned. Surely not an emergency...not now of all times. "She claims she has checked my record and found I am due at least two months leave. Effectively immediately." She grinned. "I knew the old battleaxe had a heart in there somewhere."

No sooner had they resumed their seats than the phone rang again. "That is bloody it!" Angus almost shouted. "This bloody thing is going out the window." Nevertheless he answered and Kate could see him almost stiffen to attention. "Yes sir," he said. "So, my leave is cancelled." He paused and Kate could see the veins of anger strengthen in his neck. "Colonel, you can take this job and put it so far up your...." His voice trailed off. "Oh, I see. Yes, sir, as of now. Thank you."

He hung up and turned to Kate, who had grown ashen with disbelief. How could the fates be so cruel? She looked at Angus, who instead of throwing items around the apartment was glowing with excitement. The bastard, she thought again, how could he be happy about what was obviously a further, dangerous mission?

"Kate, my love," Angus began, and then his voice broke. He cleared his throat and began again. "Kate, my darling." Here it comes, Kate thought, the deeper the endearment the bigger the mission. "The Brig had cancelled my two week leave." Just bloody brilliant Kate thought, looking around for items which she herself could throw. The Waterford champagne glass looked like a good place to start. Followed by the bottle, aimed squarely at Angus' head.

"My leave is now indefinite. It seems I have been doing too good a job training up these ranger blokes and there's no further need for my services. The Old Bastard's exact words were 'don't call us, we'll call you'." Angus shouted with laughter and collapsed onto the sofa, holding Kate as if there was indeed no tomorrow, instead of the long future together stretching before them.

Kate was weeping, with joy. "No more soldier boy," she gently teased him. "Mothballs for uniforms will be my first order for Joshua," Angus firmly stated.

He kissed Kate, long, deeply and with all the emotion he could muster on this emotional day, then rose and went to the sound system, replacing the music with a new album from an emerging Canadian poet/musician, one Leonard Cohen.

As the strains of *Hallelujah* drifted through the apartment, they made slow and gentle love on the sofa, building with the crescendo of the song through to a climax which left them both physically and emotionally drained.

"I like this Cohen fellow," Kate eventually murmured. "He has his moments," Angus agreed, and entwined they fell into a deep and warm slumber together, but not before Kate whispered in Angus' ear: "Do the speakers extend to the bedroom?" Angus smiled and kissed the tip of her nose. "For you, my lady, they will stretch from HillView to the Pool"

Chapter Seventeen

It was almost a carnival atmosphere in the car on the way to the farm. Kate's hand rested firmly high on Angus' thigh as he pushed Jonathon's BMW along at a speed he was sure his father had never posted.

This time, though, there was no bypassing the Colonial Inn. Angus motored discreetly around the back and parked under a shade tree. Next to the river, there was a private table, surrounded by flowering scrubs and laid out with silverware and, co-incidentally, a bottle of chilled Moet in an ice-bucket. Angus had called ahead and told Jurgen to pull out all stops.

Kate was suitable impressed. "This is beautiful," she murmured, as Jurgen appeared with the crayfish starter. "Thank you, ma'am," Jurgen beamed. Slimy bugger, Angus thought, then grinned at the publican.

"Good to see you again, man," he told Jurgen. "Been too long." Too long by far, Jurgen agreed and respectfully backed away, leaving them in isolated peace. It was a beautiful day and slowly they ate their way through the seemingly endless courses, topped off with another bottle of champagne.

Kate looked at Angus and Angus looked at Kate. Another private place for their new life. Words were scarcely necessary and, indeed, hardly spoken. "I hope we can come back here often," Kate eventually said.

"As often as we like," Angus smiled. "And this is our private table. Nobody else allowed here."

"How do you manage that?," Kate asked, surprised. Then her mouth twitched in a slight smile. "Of course...because the bloody Dunrows own this hotel. I should have known." Angus acknowledged her perception with a raised glass as a toast. The Dunrows in fact owned most of the businesses in Mbelo.

"Better get used to it, my sweeting," he said. Kate stared at him for a moment, not quite sure of his meaning and getting no clue from Angus' open, but inscrutable face. The only give-away, really, was the laughter in his eyes. "But now, I think we'd better trot along to the farm before Matilda really works herself into a lather. She sounded quite excited yesterday when I told her we were coming home." In fact, over the scratchy telephone line, Matilda had been ecstatically happy. Not the least that her boy had finally come up with the goods, she hoped, in the relationship stakes. But Kate had noticed the *we* and for a moment felt a little taken aback. Was Angus assuming too much, too soon? She looked at him closely again and was suddenly struck by the lightning bolt of realisation that, yes, it *was* we coming home. She'd never really had much of a home before. Her father, Uncle Tom, had been pretty rough and ready, always affectionate but had probably longed for a son. Then the terrs had burned him out.

The time in South Africa had been a succession of shared flats with other nurses, tangles of feminine underwear constantly underfoot and secret signs left on doors if privacy was desired. The nurses' quarters at the hospital hardly counted as more than a place to doss between shifts and she had with determination in her heart left Angus' flat when she sense he had drifted away.

Now there was HillView beckoning. She had always loved the farm and longed for the chance to further explore the vast ranges. She had heard that in one isolated section, near swampy land, there were even elephants and rhino. That, she knew, was strictly private information because of the fear of poachers still operating despite the war.

Within twenty minutes they pulled into the HillView driveway. Matilda, who had been looking out the window for them for the best part of the afternoon, came bustling out in full flight and, ignoring Angus gathered Kate in a huge mama-hug. "You beautiful girl, you have come back...ah we have so missed you." Kate gasped for breath and tried to smile. Matilda turned to Angus and regarded him with mock-seriousness. "As for you, Angie, it's about time!"

Kate once again felt overcome by the whirlwind that seemed to have overtaken her life. It all seemed so ... so taken for granted, she realised.

"Steady, 'Tilda, steady," Angus said the exactly right words at the right time and Kate felt her gratitude towards her man grow even further. "Kate is here to see whether she likes HillView. She may not...the cooking, for one thing, may need improvement."

Matilda stared at Angus in disbelief, and then roared with laughter. She threw her great arms around him and, to Kate's disbelief, actually lifted him off the ground and she shook with mirth.

Not to outdone, Tom appeared from around the corner of the house and performed his welcoming leap with the massive paws first on Angus, driving him back a step and then with Kate, although Angus noticed, with a great deal more gentility. Dog was simply given a friendly slap across his massive head with an equally massive paw.

Kate immediately felt relaxed and almost absurdly happy. This *was* a homecoming. On the stoep an afternoon tea of cakes, scones with cream and jam and small sandwiches was laid out, in case the twenty-minute drive from the Colonial had induced starvation.

They snacked, then entered the huge house and Angus led Kate to the bedroom wing. "This, my darling, shall be your room," he said, indicating a large bedroom which also had a private courtyard and its own bathroom facilities.

Kate was still for a moment then looked at Angus in disbelief. "What exactly do you mean by *my* room," she flared, almost stamping her foot. "What has happened to *our* room? Do you think I have come all the way here to sleep by myself? Are you totally out of your bloody mind?"

A lesser man than Angus would have quavered at the furousity in Kate's manner. But Angus was made of sterner stuff. He walked to a door set in a side wall and opened it. "This, on the other hand is *my* room. As you can see, the bed is plenty big enough for two...well maybe four if you count Tom and Dog."

Kate stared at him and began to laugh. "If you think for one moment I am sharing a bed with Tom and Dog you are out of your tiny mind, mister," she managed between chuckles. "One monster in the bed with me is all that is allowed."

"Ah well," Angus shrugged off his attempt at humour. "Even here, some proprieties have to be kept. Just ruffle your sheets from time to time to keep Gideon happy. Gives the lazy bugger something to do. Nobody, from Jonathon and Elizabeth down expects us to lead a monastic life."

There was HillView to explore, Angus mounted on Nelson and Kate on her filly, Sunshine. Together they rode endless miles, with Angus showing Kate the special places...the small cove set into a hillside where once he had shot out a leopard which had developed a taste for beef. There was the Hill itself and Kate discovered another side to the Dunrow empire. Set into the side of the Hill was a portal, the entrance to a shaft tunnelling deep into the depths. Razor wire protected the perimeter and there were no fewer than four armed guards to add to the security.

"Gold," Angus explained. "Good, rich high grade country gold. Inside," he pointed to the entrance, "there are six men working the stopes. We work slowly and carefully to make sure we get it all, but this mine has been running for twenty years and the ore shows no signs of cutting out. Word, of course, has got out and we have had a few lucrative offers from big companies.

"But, they would go in with their own modern methods. Major excavations, a treatment plant clunking away day and night. We like it the way it is – Daniel and I spent one summer holiday working in there. It's not for the faint hearted, but these men get paid extremely well."

"Gold," Kate wondered aloud. "Next you will be showing me the Dunrow Diamond Mine!"

Angus chuckled. "You never know," and gave her a look of deep significance. "Might find a use for a large one," he added with a wink. The look, wink and words were totally lost on Kate who was totally absorbed as men filed out of the shaft and there was the distant rumble of explosive from within the mine. Angus checked his watch. "One o'clock...blasting time. Also lunch time for the miners until the dust has settled and been watered down." He didn't repeat the diamond statement...somehow the moment had passed. They rode around the front of the Hill, to the Pool for their own luncheon special, as Angus had come to refer to their regular trysts on the picnic blanket by the water. From the first time together, at another pool, it had never lost the magic.

Then one day Angus announced: "Pack some tough bush gear together – there's plenty your size in my sister's closet, help yourself. I hope you agree," he concluded, "but I think it's long overtime we went on safari. Get away from here for a couple or few weeks, out in the bush where very few people have been, even now."

"Are we taking Dog?" Kate enquired. Actually, a safari sounded wonderful. She realised, with surprise, she had now been at HillView for almost two months and although now firmly entrenched there and treated as one of the family she looked forward to a longer break.

"Of course," Angus replied, surprised.

"In that case, I shall feel safe," Kate replied. "Rather than relying on a large, sometimes smelly man who has been known to drink too much gin around a campfire." It was a terrible injustice and Angus affected a sense of wounded pride. "I shall also take a few cases of beer for Dog in that case," he retorted.

The preparation for the safari was straight-forward, honed by years of similar expeditions, first with Jonathon and later with Daniel. Food trunks, well-worn but also well-maintained camping gear, photographic equipment, a long-range fuel tank and lastly, weapons. Kate raised her eyebrows at Angus over that decision. Not once in the time since they had been at HillView had he touched a gun.

"Just in case," Angus answered the unspoken question. Guns could be used for more than defence against the ungodly. Often bushmeat made a welcome change to the safari rations. But not once had Angus mentioned the war, although they listened every night to the BBC World Service on the radio for propaganda-free updates. The situation, it seemed, was growing more grim with each passing month.

The gear was carefully stowed in the LandRover, along with essential spare mechanical parts, and they were set to set off. The next morning at first light was the choice. Angus wanted to reach a particularly favourite location by early afternoon. It would be an arduous and adventurist drive through some breathtaking countryside.

Matilda had breakfast sizzling for them as they sat in the pre-dawn chill, with layers of clothes on. "We layer up in the morning and layer down as the day gets warmer," he explained to Kate, who had questioned why she could not simply wear her voluminous wool sweater.

Angus drove sedately for the first couple of kilometres, both to allow the engine to warm and to test for any last-minute mechanical hitches. Then he pushed the pedal to the metal and the Rover roared forward. It would only be for the first thirty kilometres, Angus knew, for after that lay just rough bush tracks, where they existed at all, or simply scrub-bashing. That was the part he most enjoyed, far from civilisation and just the occasional bush-village, where life still went on following centuries-old tradition.

The day had warmed once they reached the bush itself and the layer-theory of clothing began to make sense to Kate. As they navigated rough semi-tracks and more than once cut through virgin bush, she looked at Angus more often. She realised she had not seen him so relaxed and at peace within himself for a long,

long time. He spoke little, except to point out occasional wildlife which Kate otherwise would have missed, for the animals' natural camouflage blended perfectly into their native surroundings.

"There's plenty more ahead," Angus promised as she protested when he refused to stop for photographs. "More than you can imagine."

By noon the scenery had changed again, the veldt giving way to more hilly and forested countryside. Only once did Angus stop, cutting the motor and coasting to a halt just short of a sleepy glade with a small clearing. He put his mouth close to Kate's ear and whispered "lion", pointing to the far end of the clearing. Kate stared for a moment, then the scenario sprung into sharp focus. There were three lionesses she could see, supervising a bundle of excited cubs falling over each other as they mock-fought...and a dozing lion clearly keeping his distance from the hurly-burly.

Angus collected his photographic gear from its bag and carefully fitted a telephoto lens to the Canon. Just as silently, he climbed over the Rover's door and stalked towards the pack. He had already judged the slight breeze would not carry his man-smell towards it. Kate suddenly felt very alone. Angus appeared to have just disappeared into the bush, but just minutes later he reappeared just as silently, with a grin of triumph on his face.

"Beautiful," he breathed. "Just beautiful." He restarted the motor and they boxed around the lion pack before continuing west.

"Why didn't they pay us any attention," Kate demanded. "They must have known we were there?"

"These are animals in the wild with no contact with humans, except for the odd tribesman, who would give them a wide berth," Angus explained. "So they have no reason to associate us with danger. You noticed they showed no agitation? Closer to home, they would have been long gone before we got anywhere near, or formed into a defensive pack, the lionesses in particular guarding their cubs. Of course," he added, "you can never tell – one of them might have had a toothache, or a thorn in the paw and was feeling grumpy."

"You, Angus Dunrow," Kate smiled at him, "Are a complete bastard! You left me sitting there not knowing where you were, by myself, with a pack of lions within rock-throwing distance."

"Ah," Angus said. "But I knew precisely where *you* were and I was between you and the lions every step of the way."

"And armed with nothing but a camera," Kate continued. "What were you going to do...throw it at them?"

"Waste of a good camera," Angus nonchantly replied. "I would have shouted and waved my hat at them. Usually works."

"Usually?" Kate said. "That *usually* works?"

"Usually," Angus confirmed and drove on, tunelessly whistling 'When the Lion Feeds Tonight'. He smiled to himself. Already this safari was turning out well and the best to yet to come. Another hour of picking their way through the increasingly forested terrain and the ground began to change again, this time to a blacker soil with abundant wildflowers. Angus selected a campsite with care and pulled over. "Home, sweet home...for tonight," he explained and set about pitching camp. Normally he and Jonathon or Daniel would have slept rough on the ground with just a blanket, but in deference to Kate, Angus had included a spacious tent in the kit, along with stretcher beds and even a fold-up bedside table, with lanterns for the darkness.

A dining table followed next, with comfortable camp chairs and Angus built a fire site in anticipation of the chilly night to come.

"It's wonderful," Kate said with sincerity, looking around. "But why stop here? It's barely lunchtime." A problem Angus was solving with fresh meat from the chilled food trunk.

"It's time to do what the animals do in the middle of the day," he explained. "Siesta time. Later, near sunset, I'll take you to a pool just nearby, where if we're lucky we'll see all types of game." Including elephant, he secretly hoped, but that really was pushing their luck on the first day out. Sometime in the next two or so weeks, he knew he could guarantee Kate an encounter with the monster animals, with which Angus had been fascinated since early childhood. He'd studied them, both up close and from any reference book on the beasts he could find. He was particularly interested in their intra-herd communications and the aunty elephants, who would discipline any wayward and rambunctious calves with a sapling branch. He also appreciated the behaviour of the male boss elephant, who would appear from his solitary ramblings when the females came into season and, duty done, wander off on their own again, leaving the younger males to mock-fight for supremacy. Henry Mancini's 1962 music Baby Elephant Walk was indelibly etched in Angus' mind.

Two hours before dark he and Kate set off, on foot, with a ration pack mainly containing water and dried biscuits. Angus also carried a heavy rifle. Dog was ordered to stay and guard the camp, a duty he filled with obvious reluctance. They moved through the forest, Kate carefully observing how silently Angus moved and trying to emulate him, for any twig she stepped on cracked, drawing an irritated look from Angus. She briefly thought of where Angus had learned most of his cat-like bushcraft and silently shuddered.

Finally they paused at the top of a small hillock overlooking a breathtakingly beautiful pond about the size of a half-Olympic swimming pool. It was full from recent rains and there were heavily-marked tracks surrounding the trodden-down perimeter. Angus settled into a comfortable, but hidden position with a clear view of the pond and motioned Kate to join him. He readied his camera and whispered "now we wait. Shouldn't be too long".

It seemed just five minutes later the first antelope cautiously approached the water, warily sniffing the air for potential predators. Within moments he was joined by several other kudus, who drank their fill and then as one filtered back into the bush. Angus had shot several photographs and changed the roll of film. Now he nudged Kate and motioned with his hand to the left of the pool. A giraffe was coming in. Kate almost giggled as he bent into the ridiculous knock-kneed pose giraffes are forced to adopt when drinking. Even Angus smiled, but waited for several moments before the camera whirred again. He had been anticipating the perfect moment for the last of the sun to light up the Southern

Giraffe's colours. A giraffe can drink twelve gallons of water in one go, but can also last for days without. This particular chap was also keeping a wary eye out for its two major predators, lion and crocodiles. As far as Angus knew, there were no crocs here, but he wouldn't be taking a swim to prove he was right.

Just as the light was fading completely, Kate sensed Angus tense beside her and he pointed in another direction as he quickly loaded low-speed film into the Canon and loaded the F-stop into its lowest position. With the dwindling light it was possible he could get a "keeper" of a shot. An elephant casually wandered out of the surrounding foliage and began drinking his fill. He also allowed himself the luxury of squirting water back over his shoulders. Not an old chap, Angus saw, barely about seven years' old, but with a promising set of tusks which, nature and poachers allowing, would grow impressively over the next fifty or so years. Apart from man, grown elephants had no predators.

He placed the camera back in the bag. It was too dark now for effective photography and he even doubted the ones he had managed would be workable. Perhaps with some darkroom magic he thought, philosophically. But it was a wonderful portent. He was now positive they would see plenty more of the world's largest land mammal in the coming days.

He glanced at Kate. Her face was shining with excitement and her eyes glittered as if she had seen some prize...which Angus realised she had. She had never been so close to wild game in her life, in their natural state. Silently he cheered for her. Aloud, now, he said: "And that concludes tonight's entertainment." He leaned and kiss her smiling mouth..."well, for now anyway."

Chapter Eighteen

They pressed on further into the more mountainous area before finally reaching a plateau from which a huge natural depression in the terrain revealed a massive swamp-like area, covered with ponds and dense forestation.

Angus stopped the vehicle at a beautiful site for their camp tonight. "This is as far as we drive," he told Kate. "From tomorrow it's shanks' pony. No vehicles allowed in here.

"This is the far end of our property, the farming and grazing proptery, now is the beginning or our private wildlife reserve. Here I can guarantee you everything in the African wild...including some of the biggest crocs you'll come across. They bask on the banks during the day and slip into the shallows at feeding time, when their scoff comes to drink."

"You *own* this?" Kate asked incredulously. "And I'm not so sure about walking around with crocs all over the place"

And that was why Angus had the heavy gun, he explained. "Shooting's not allowed either, except of course for poachers, who have learned the hard way not to come here. There's a group of rangers here full time to keep things in order, you'll meet them tomorrow. Along with elephant, buffalo, hippos and all the rest. This place is a haven – in fact, that's we call it. You're joining a very select few who have been invited here."

Kate was honoured, she said, once again covertly examining Angus. His strength was back in full and here, in the wilderness she sensed a freedom surrounding him. He was, she realised again, a true native of Africa.

They left in the early morning as the sun was just rising over the horizon. Descending into the haven she immediately noticed the change in the natural environment. She lost count of the number of rare birds, lion packs and herds of hippo they passed, giving each a respectful distance.

They stopped by a natural pond for lunch, cold rations of bully-beef and unleavened bread, washed down with the pure water from a nearby spring. Kate felt her own senses lift.

"I have never been anywhere quite so beautiful," she quietly murmured to Angus. "It's no wonder you keep it private."

"It's a place of harmony," Angus agreed. "I come here by myself sometimes and can wander around for a week and still not see it all. And each time there's a new surprise – a new family of lion, some cheetah which have found themselves in seventh heaven and decided to stay put."

"Do you ever have to use that?" Kate pointed to the rifle with more than a trace of disapproval. This was a place of serenity, not to be tainted by the roar of gunfire.

"Never," Angus said. "Mostly I don't bother bringing it... but," he grinned, "This time I have valuable cargo with me and he leaned and kissed her. "By the way...there's something I've been meaning to ask you for some time...". His tone was so serious Kate looked at him in bewilderment, once again struck by Angus' ability to change moods in mid sentence.

Angus coughed a trifle nervously and reached into his backpack, drawing out a small, beautifully-wrapped box. "I was wondering, well hoping, no...praying that one day it could come to this." He suddenly went silent.

Kate looked at him in bewilderment, then at the small box. She started to feel a tingling which started at her feet and spread up until her cheeks turned a rosy reddish hue. "Just blurt it out, whatever it is, you bastard of a man," she whispered.

"Kate Hansen," Angus began, then stopped and cleared his throat.

"Will you do me the greatest honour, the highest point in my life ...

"Will you marry me?"

Tears flooded down Kate's cheeks and she felt faint for a moment. This was the moment for which she had been longing. And Angus, unerringly had chosen the precisely right time and right place. She fell, crying openly now, into Angus' arms and kissed him with every ounce of passion she had built for this man, passion she knew with certainty was returned in full. The rest of her life with this beautiful but contradictory man, a man capable deep sensitivity yet hardened by the reality of the Rhodesia in which they now lived.

"Yes," she murmured into Angus' ear. "A thousand times, yes!"

Angus held her in a bear grip which betrayed his relief...and anxiety over her answer. He gave her the small box, which Kate gently opened. It contained the most beautiful diamond Kate had ever imagined, set in a magnificent crafted ring. She slipped it on the appropriate finger to find it was a perfect fit. It was, of course, a Dunrow diamond set in Dunrow gold. The effect was overwhelming.

"Kate Dunrow..." she mused aloud...."Do you know, I love the sound of that already!"

"There's only one thing missing..." Angus looked at her, then smiled and reached into the backpack, withdrawing a chilled bottle from the ice box back at their camp. Veuve Clicquot, from an outstanding vintage and one which had received a Royal Warrant bestowed by Elizabeth, Queen of England. "Good enough for the Queen, barely adequate for you," he smiled.

The rest of the afternoon was taken up by celebratory love-making, each possessing the other with passionate heights they had never before scaled. At last Angus looked at the sun and made a decision. Dog, who had been looking on with tolerant humour, suddenly arose, knowing the tone of Angus' voice meant movement.

"We'd better make a move on now," he said. "Unless you fancy being croc-grub tonight....which would seem a shame before the ceremony." Kate punched him, none too gently, in the ribs.

"Just because I agreed, in a weak moment, to marry you does not give you the right to tease me," she argued, but with a smile on her face. she reconsidered. "But you wouldn't be you if you didn't, so this time you are forgiven."

They gathered up their kit and moved further into the swamp, towards a distant small ridge visible just a couple of kilometres away. And despite their luggage burden, they held hands and stopped every so often for a break...and a kiss. Angus reflected to himself he had never been more content, happier or felt so full of life. With Kate beside him in life, there was little more he could wish for. Even the images of the war were blocked out.

As the climbed the ridge, Kate saw the outlines of a log cabin, which resembled a barracks built in a U-shape around a tended natural grass lawn and a large braai pit, with several chairs and tables scattered around.

There were also five Black men sitting there, sipping what were obviously their sundowner beers. They were tough-looking specimens, yet unusually quiet and conversed in low tones, although there were plenty of chuckles between them. The fire in the braai pit was starting to blaze and it would an hour or so before it had sufficiently settled to start cooking the evening meal. They rose as one as they saw Angus and greeted him in Sindebele, each offering the traditional African handshake. Angus introduced Kate as his bride-to-be and was met with broad beams of approval and a few ribald comments in Sindebele.

"Yes, I hope I will bear many sons and my breasts and hips are perfect for child-rearing," she told them fluently in their own language. There was a pause of deep embarrassment and the men shuffled their toes in the dust, which had suddenly gained their intense interest. Then one began laughing and such was the infectious joy of it that immediately everyone joined in, including Kate herself and Angus.

They settled themselves in spare chairs and joined in the chat. Angus was particularly pleased to hear there had been no poacher incursions and between them the rangers, all former Leopards, were covering most of the haven each day. The meat roasting on the braai was ready and Angus and Kate partook of the meal with undisguised relish.

Kate suddenly had a thought. "If no vehicles are allowed, how did all this get here?" she asked, pointing to the barracks.

"Tractor," Angus replied. "And trailer, of course. There's a muddy old track coming in from the back. Actually," he stretched himself. "There is more accommodation, for family use. Come on." He shouldered both packs and led Kate down a path about a hundred metres, where a beautifully-crafted cottage blended into the surrounding trees. It was picture-perfect, with a wide stoep at front from which to enjoy the fading sunshine.

Inside was designed being functional, but Kate could detect the hand of Elizabeth in the furnishings and decorations. Large sofas fronted onto a huge fireplace built from country rock and the walls were covered with magnificent blown-up wildlife photographs. She didn't need to question Angus as to the identity of the photographer – the work was distinctly his, with uncanny balance of subjects, ranging from hippos to elephant to exotic birdlife, enhanced by the unique natural beauty of the haven.

It was absolutely idyllic, Kate thought, as she grew to love her soon-to-be husband even more than she'd thought possible. Angus himself had blossomed and she saw many more sides to her man than she thought possible.

He could argue with her over a point of philosophy to the early hours with an easy banter, or have her in fits of laughter with a wide collection of often ribald jokes and cynical one-liners which occasionally she caught onto some time later and would start chuckling for no apparent reason.

And he had opened entirely with her, sharing his most intimate details and desires. One subject which remained off the agenda, however, was the war. The haven was just that – a place not to be sullied by the ugliness of the country's sufferings.

They lived largely off the land, Angus taking a light rifle from the heavily-fortified gun safe and quickly and compassionately despatching a choice impala, of which there were hundreds. There was no sport in the business. Angus would simply creep to a suitable firing position and take down the quarry. Other necessities also came from the haven, as Angus pointed out edible and often delicious berries and other plants and cooked them with his own hand. A man of many parts, Kate thought more than once.

Their love-making, always just a casual glance away, became yet more tumultuous. And often at the drop of a hat, or more appropriately their pants, as Angus once wryly observed after a particularly torrid time way out into the haven.

They made plans for the wedding. "Better be prepared for the whole shebang," Angus had winced as he'd said it. "Myself, a registrar in Bulawayo and a couple of chaps off the street as witnesses would do the trick." And that had sparked a blazing row, where words such as unromantic bastard and uncaring chauvinist had been flung at him.

"And I suppose the reception would be in the front bar of the Elephant and Lion," Kate had shouted. Angus had shrugged: "At least the beer is cold there." Until Kate had noticed the mischievous glint in his eyes and realised that, once again, he had successfully baited her. That had earned Angus another hefty belt in the ribs.

Eventually, though, it was time to end the safari and head back to civilisation. Kate counted and to her surprise found they had been away from HillView for more than six weeks. "Yes," she had sighed...it's time to return to reality." Then she remembered they were returning as a couple shortly to be joined forever and her female instincts kicked in with glee as she thought of the list of people to be informed...Jonathon, Elizabeth, Daniel and Sally, her nursing friends. She smiled. She would even invite Matron as a guest – after all, the old battleaxe had played more than her fair share in bringing her and Angus together. Angus, for his part, casually mentioned they could expect about 500 guests. The wedding itself, of course, would be held in the beautiful grounds at HillView.

Casually, totally without haste, they made their way out of the haven, first bidding a fond farewell to the rangers, who had not only kept a very discreet distance, but also provided titbits of delicious food – mainly wild geese, turkey and birds on the wing. The roasted wild pigeon was particularly delicious.

They made it back to the LandRover on the third day and decided not to dally, loading their supplies and taking the rough tracks towards HillView. Angus drove at a more sedate pace, avoiding the worst of the potholes and outcrops and glancing constantly at Kate to ensure her comfort.

For Kate had delivered the earth-shattering news just as they were about to leave the cottage in the haven. Casually she had curled into Angus' lap and smiled her secret smile to him.

"Angus, darling, I'm late...and I have never been late in my life." It took Angus a full minute to decipher her meaning. "You mean...." and his voice trailed off.

"Unless I'm very much mistaken, and I am a nurse, remember," Kate confirmed. "I'm pregnant."

The unbridled joy which sprang from Angus was intoxicating. They were laughing and talking over each other, but of one thing Kate was sure...Angus was going to make an outstanding father. Mind you, he had to grow up a bit first, but the makings were there.

"You're going to have a baby!" He exclaimed more than once. "Correction, Dunrow," Kate had replied. "*We* are going to have a baby."

"We'd better organise the wedding bloody quickly then," Angus had finally managed. "Invitations go out at once." Which had earned him another punch, this time on the shoulder.

"You don't need to get so practical so bloody soon," Kate said. "Besides which," and she started to nuzzle his ear..."I have a much better idea for right now."

Chapter Nineteen

Tom was the first to greet them as they drove up to the Hillview home, leisurely dropping down from his favourite branch and sauntering over to the Rover, where he scratched his side along the body work, then put his huge paws over the door still. He looked at Angus as if to query his absence and, if it were at all possible, Angus could have sworn he smiled at Kate.

Tom was closely followed by Elizabeth, who in turn was bustled along by Matilda. "Tom knew you were coming yesterday," she smiled as she hugged first Angus then Kate. Dog received a friendly cuff from Tom. "Welcome home..." she stepped back and appraised them both. "Looks like you both found a wonderful time out there." She glanced at the height of the sun. "Time for elevens", as she led them onto the stoep.

"Actually Ma..." Angus began and shuffled his boot in the dust. He looked at the house as if he'd never seen it before, then at Matilda who was staring at him with unabashed curiosity. She'd never seen Angus nervous before and she realised momentious news must be forthcoming. Elizabeth had also stopped and was staring at Angus with maternal curiosity. Most unlike her son, she thought.

Angus cleared his throat, then glanced at Katey, by his side. Suddenly he relaxed and laughed, a deep chuckle. He put his arm around Kate's shoulder. "I have asked this beautiful lady to marry me and much against her common sense she has agreed."

He smiled at Elizabeth, a radiant gesture which changed to an "oomph" as Elizabeth rushed him and hugged first him then Kate, then both at once. Matilda was half a pace behind, beaming from ear to ear.

"Finally," Matilda managed. "Finally you have grown some sense." Huge tears of joy ran down her copious cheeks. "You are now my daughter as well," she said to Kate.

Elizabeth took Kate by the hand and led her to the table, calling over her shoulder for champagne. "Welcome to the family," she said. "I can't tell you how happy this makes me and Jonathon will be delighted. I'll call him this evening. Meantime we have plans to make!"

Matilda had held back a little from the group and had been surreptitiously studying Kate. Now she smiled. "I think there is more news yet," she said knowingly. Kate and Angus both blanched, but Matilda went on. "Something as important?"

Elizabeth turned her eye to Kate, but it was Angus who answered. "Well..." started bravely and then stalled and stopped. "Well...."

"Oh for God's sake, Angus," Kate snapped. She smiled serenely to Elizabeth. "I am pregnant."

"Two for price of one," Angus sheepishly admitted, but his mumbled comment was drowned by Elizabeth's cry of joy and she came around the table and swept Kate into her arms.

Matilda broke into more tears of joy and crushed Angus to her bosom. "My warrior," she whispered into his ear. The champagne came and Angus did the honours, pausing momentarily before Kate. Somewhere in the past he had heard of pregnant ladies and alcohol, but after that he was quite foggy on the subject.

"Just one glass, Angus," Kate teased him. "I am sure Elizabeth had one or two when she had you as her burden." Elizabeth smiled and touched glasses with Kate. "One or two, my dear..just one or two. Although he fought so much in there a bottle or two would have been preferable....as for the birth..." she trailed off and Angus, puce with embarrassment, drained his glass in one swallow and muttered something about getting the Matabeland mud off him and disappeared inside the house. It was scarcely noticed. Kate had the full attention of both Elizabeth and Matilda.

Had Angus stayed, he would have been privy to the worst-kept secret in the wedding world. When it comes to the matrimonial moment, the groom is surplus to requirements. He must appear, sober as possible, mumble "I do" a couple of times and then leave the rest of the day to the bride. After that, he gets kisses from all the female guests and hearty handshakes and slaps on the back from the lads.

So he wandered into his room and took full advantage of the hot shower, staying in for long minutes as the water rinsed off the accumulated muck. His clothes he threw into a corner...they could be incinerated later.

Angus came from the ablutions feeling surprisingly refreshed. Which was not all that surprising, he guessed. He had just had the best time of his life with Kate in the bush, gained a wife-to-be and....and a child.

He grinned at his reflection in the bedroom mirror. "Not bad going, man," he said aloud and sat heavily on the bed, disturbing Tom who had already assumed residence. "You will have to find alternative accommodation soon, my old son," he sternly told Tom. Tom's response was a massive yawn and to roll over to let his stomach be scratched.

The wedding came and went without a hitch. In just three weeks, Elizabeth had made all the arrangements. There were 300 invited guests, including Prime Minister Ian Smith. He had made special arrangements for a helicopter to arrive at Hillview on time, but had warned Elizabeth he couldn't stay for the fest ivies.

All the guests were greeted with glasses of champagne or harder liquor if they preferred. As well as the 300 invited guests, there were at least 500 local Matabele people, from farms and townships nearby. They had heard the news and each had a special attachment to the Dunrow family. Had they not provided food when they were hungry? Money when times were hard and their children needed school books? Employment when then was nothing around to care for their families? The Dunrows may have been very rich, but they cared for their people. Now they gathered at the fringes of the invited guests, in a quiet silence as in reverence. Nkomo Angus. Marrying. Unfortunately for the only time they knew. A man needed at least three wives to be content.

The guests were all seated when Angus strode down the make-shift isle to the altar, which was chaired by the Bishop of Bulawayo....a gentleman of wide-ranging views who frequently argued with anyone who opposed his point of view of democracy. A controversial man, with whom Angus had frequently clashed on points of philosophy ... but a man Angus deeply admired.

Angus was dressed in full uniform and for once had all his medals displayed. Once again he lost an argument with both his mother and Kate. He would have preferred a simple black-tie affair. But, then he reminded himself, as Daniel, similarly attired, walked with him as the Best Man His job was to simply be the groom. This day belonged to Kate. The rest of their lives belonged to both of them.

Back in their room at last, the hour way past midnight, the last guests snoring in their bedrolls or having left earlier to avoid ambush time – darkness – Angus held Kate close. "There is one question left," he murmured to her. "Where do you fancy our honeymoon? South Africa...Madagascar...England?"

Kate, close to sleep herself, rolled more into Angus' arms. "We have already had our honeymoon, my love." She rubbed her hands down Angus' back. "And you have already knocked me up. I am having our baby....it must be here. This is our home."

Our home it was to be, indeed. The next morning Elizabeth sent Angus off to check on a few cattle she thought were looking poorly, and then joined Kate on the veranda for morning tea. "Of course I will be moving out," she said. "A house can only have one mistress." Kate immediately began to object, but Elizabeth smoothly over-road her. "Also, I get very lonely here by myself.... with Jonathon away so much, I shall shift to Salisbury to our house there to be near him. I know the poor chap gets lonely as well."

Chapter Twenty

The inevitable call came eventually, as both Angus and Daniel feared it would.

The political situation had further deteriorated with talks in far-off London producing few positive results so far. The fighting was intensifying, with the terrorists using increasingly sophisticated weapons and coming closer to the major cities. Eleven shoppers were killed and seventy injured in a bombing attack on Woolworths department store in Salisbury itself.

The Prime Minister was bowing to pressure from abroad and announced majority rule within two years, but at the same time stepping up the military battle with ZANLA and ZIPRA militants, hoping to cut down their numbers while launching a 'hearts and minds' programme among the black landowners and business people.

The call came from the Brig himself. Harry Johnson was brief, to the point and left no room for misunderstanding. "You're leave is cancelled as of now," he told Angus. You and Nkumo report for duty immediately." Then he softened somewhat. "Sorry, Angus, but we have a big one coming up and we need both of you right there at the fire face."

Angus had profusely cursed and sworn after the call ended. He was a farmer now, for God's sake. His war days, and those of Daniel, had seemed well behind them. So it was in a foul mood he broke the news to Kate.

He had expected Kate to throw one of her now-legendary tantrums. With the rapidly advancing pregnancy had come sudden mood changes. But she accepted the news quietly, although with tears in her eyes.

"You poor man," she embraced Angus. "We were doing so well. I have never seen you happier." Angus was indeed trembling, both with rage and in fearful anticipation of life back in uniform. He felt as if the earth had crumbled beneath his feet. Three days' time and he would be back with the Leopards going to face God-knew-what back out in the bush. But he knew the war from which he and Daniel had successfully insulated themselves, raged on with atrocities being committed by both sides.

Daniel was no less antagonised by the order. He and Angus had built something special in their joint ventures, which included security consulting for several farms in nearby areas designing and overseeing defence strategies.

Sally was also furious. "How much more can they expect from you?" she had exploded. "You have given everything to them already. Refuse! Tell them to go and jump..." and then broken down into a tearful mess. Daniel held her close.

"I have to go," he sadly told her. "We cannot live in a fool's paradise forever. Our men are dying out there," he reasoned, both for his own sake and that of Sally.

He was collected two days later by Angus and Dog in the LandRover and in silence they drove to Bulawayo, to the barracks and Leopard headquarters, where they were quietly welcomed back by the Colonel.

"Sorry it had to come to this," he said. "But the bastards are becoming deadlier by the day. More incursions, more murderous attacks." Also fifty innocent villagers had been killed in crossfire between the armed forces and terrorists, a slaughter for which each side blamed the other. The solution, it had been decided, was to the send the Special Forces out in number. The Leopards' brief remained the same – to track and destroy the terr hostiles, whether on the border or deep into Mozambique itself.

"We have a specific target for you," the Colonel continued. "It's being used as both a training and transit base for the gooks who are coming across the border. We estimate about three thousand are there now.

"The airforce are going to lead the attack, backed by your team at the fire frontline. There also will be Scouts, who have already been watching the camp, the SAS and the RLI."

Angus whistled through clenched teeth..."Why are we needed?" he inquired. "It sounds as if you have the situation well under control." He wasn't outrightly rejecting the idea, nor could he, but there seemed more to it all than met the eye.

"Your specific role is backup for the others," the Colonel fired back. "There will be some of the terrs who will get away. They may be wounded, but they will flee. Most, of course, will be armed ... scared and dangerous. You watch the SAS and RLI's backs and take care of any who slip through the net."

Angus nodded. "Where exactly is this base," he asked. The Colonel told him the co-ordinates and Angus' quick calculation put it roughly sixty kilometres inside the Mozambique border. Similar missions had been successfully carried out before, with no air support.

"There will be a decoy old DC3 fly over the base first up," the Colonel said. "They will think it is just a normal reconnaissance flight, especially when it turns around, flies back and keeps on track for the Rhodesian border. With luck, they will think little of it – just we are gathering more intelligence to gauge their state of readiness. But suddenly the aerial attack aircraft appear, at low altitude with all guns blazing and napalm being dropped, along with more than a few bombs. That is when the SAS and RLI move in. So, in short, you are the backstop and add additional fire when appropriate."

"How are the troops getting in?" Angus asked. "Sixty kilometres through hostile country with guards and checkpoints all along every route...that's dangerous ground."

"Ah," the Colonel replied. "That's also part of your job, which I haven't yet mentioned. Leopards will go in two days earlier, tabbing it through and taking out as many as possible along the way. Most of the troops, however, will 'chute in – but they need an exit route for the way home."

Angus nodded understanding. Suddenly the Leopards' role became crystal clear...as did the reason why the group itself had been chosen. Long range aggressive missions were their forte. Two days, however, was cutting it fine.

"Two things," he said. "Make it three days earlier so we can make sure of the job without alerting those further in – wet, but quiet work. And secondly, why Daniel and myself? The Leopards are in capable hands now, well-led by John Robinson and Jack Berry and superbly trained."

"Whose idea was the Leopards in the first place?" the Colonel countered. "I have already spoken to John and Jack and they are happy, more than happy, to have the pair of you lead them in – and out. And the reason they are superbly trained was that you and Daniel hand-picked them and taught them the special ropes. And three days it will be, but you will have to leave a day earlier...there has been too much planning with the rest to alter their mission status."

Angus could think of no rejoinder. He knew the Leopards would be in full combat status almost immediately. They could leave at a moment's notice if necessary. "When do we go?" he asked.

"Now, with your change to the plans, the day after tomorrow. We want to hit them on Saturday, so you'll leave on Wednesday. That leaves you the rest of today and tomorrow to study the maps and plan.

Angus and Daniel, who had remained silent but ready to intervene if necessary. Angus may have mellowed, he thought, but he could still have a short fuse on his temper. But now he spoke, directly to Angus: "We'd better pull our fingers out and get moving then."

They nodded goodbye to the Colonel and headed directly to the Leopards' separate encampment. The sentry saluted as he let them through the checkpoint. "Welcome home Sah," he greeted them both individually.

Angus thought about that for a moment as they passed. Yes, he realised, this *was* home...for now. This was home for the time being, while he was protecting his own home from the escalating terrorism threat. Protecting his farm and, above all, his pregnant wife and soon-to-born baby. He would ring Kate before they left, he decided and although without detail give her more than the 'we're off again' line which had proved so unsuccessful in the past.

All the same, he found it hard to shake off a feeling of foreboding at the back of his mind. Although seemingly well-co-ordinated and planned, the best laid plans of mice and men...this was an extremely dangerous mission, of that he had no doubt. It was also more than likely there would be friendly casualties and their task was to keep those to an absolute minimum. No easy job, he thought, a feeling shared immediately by John Robinson and Jack Berry, both of whom welcomed them back with open arms.

"It's great to have you back," John said. "This is going to be a bugger of a job." He had also offered to vacant Angus' old office, an offer Angus immediately declined. They would share it, he told John, who with Jack and Daniel would refine the plan which the pair had tentatively, pending approval, drawn up.

"How much do the men know?" he asked John. John filled him in, that the Leopards knew they were once again heading into the danger zone and were combat ready. All identication had been handed in, weapons checked and rechecked and all the kit had been issued.

"They're ready," he told Angus. "We just need to know when...we already know where and why."

Angus told him the departure date, just one and a half days away and John nodded with satisfaction. "Grand," he said. "Any longer and they would start to lose the edge." Angus knew to what he was referring. Sustained readiness with no order to go in sight could be sapping to both patience and the state of mind they were building to embark into perils largely known, except it would be extremely dangerous.

"Good," he said. "We will have a full briefing tonight, complete lockdown until Wednesday morning. How many do we have?" There were always men away, some on furlough, some on missions. But all men had been recalled and would be back in camp that night, John reassured him. So, with the addition of Angus and Daniel, they had a complement of fifty-two.

"So, let's start the concrete planning right now," Angus said. "Five teams of ten each, two of which will be eleven with me and Daniel coming along. We'll go in separate routes on the way in and rendezvous five kilometres from the site. Oh...", he paused for a moment. "One of those teams will actually have twelve. Dog is a beret-wearing Leopard." The others grinned at the weak joke, but it broke the tension and they fell into detailed planning.

At six o'clock, Angus glanced at the wall clock and broke up the meeting. "Dinner now and we'll fill the blokes in at twenty hundred hours," he had already reverted to army-speech.

At eight o'clock the briefing room was packed. Angus and the other leaders took to the podium. John spoke first.

"For those of you who have joined in more recent times, this gentleman and I use the term loosely of course, is Major Angus Dunrow, who with Sergeant Major Daniel Nkumo, were founders of the Leopards. It was Angus who gave us the name in the first place.

Many of the Leopards were old hands and had previously served under Angus and Daniel. To the newcomers, neither needed much introduction. Both were Leopard legends.

"Thanks, John," Angus nodded to the man then gave the gathering his full attention. For more than an hour he used large maps and pointers to fully explain the mission to his men, who were silent as they concentrated on the enormity of the task ahead. For most, if Angus said it was do-able, that was enough for them. For the newcomers, their respect for the man on the podium grew with each passing word. Angus explained in full detail the risks, the potential rewards and the vital nature of their jobs.

"Finally," he concluded, "Are there any questions?" But such had been the detail he had imparted there were none. "Good, "Angus said. "Anybody think of any in the meantime, contact one of us immediately. We're not bulletproof, so anything you think may be worthwhile would be welcome. There are no stupid questions, just the one you don't ask."

There was a sudden silence, then something occurred which had never happened at any briefing Angus had attended or presented. The men, as one cheered, slapped each other on the back and applauded. It was unheard of, yet deeply touching and once again Angus realised how much he had treasured this elite group. And still did, perhaps even more so, he smiled to himself.

Back in the office, he excused himself and made a private call, to Kate at HillView. Without going into specific mission details, he filled Kate in as much as possible.

"We going into terr territory," he said. "This is going to be a tough one, but we can do it. Just remember one thing, my darling, I love you and our sprog and there is one promise I will never break. You already have my heart, you'll soon have the rest of me back with you at our home."

There were tears from Kate's end. Never before had Angus been so forthcoming. She was afraid for him, but knew his courage and experience gave both him and his men, including Daniel, the best chance of success.

"I love you darling Dunrow," she almost whispered down the line, which for once was free of the usual crackle and hiss which accompanied most phone calls to and from HillView. "Come back soon or I'll bloody well kill you myself!"

Angus was still smiling as he finally hung up. Amazingly the call had lifted his spirits from the doldrums and he found renewed energy to focus on the job in hand.

They plotted and planned further into the night until Angus called it a night. "Enough," he said. Let's keep it fresh. Most of the men will be having a final beer...I suggest we join them."

Chapter Twenty One

They left at dawn on Wednesday, ferried to the border by four open-top trucks, sitting back-to-back with their kits piled on the floor. Each man carried his weapon of choice, which largely was the M16, pointed outwards against possible ambush.

The teams were dropped at two kilometre-apart points as near to the border as possible, so in total twenty kilometres would be sanitised for the attackers' return route. They expected little in the way of resistance, probably sentry outposts manned by fewer than twenty men, half of whom would be sleeping at any given time.

And so it proved for the first ten kilometres into Mozambique. Of the ten teams, just three came across hostiles, who were despatched by minimal force with short bursts of gunfire and where possible by knives and garrottes. Communication lines were deliberately left untouched so as to not alert other outposts further in.

But after that the terr outposts became more frequent. Angus' group, forewarned by a growling Dog, literally stumbled across one. It was a balmy day and most of the uglies were lying dozing in the sun. At Angus' command they stealthily surrounded the group and opened fire. It was over in less than a minute. Angus knew they had taken a chance going noisy, but the time for caution was now over and they were now more than twenty kilometres inside the border. On either side of them, two kilometres more or less depending on the terrain, the other Leopards would have heard the brief gunfire and recognized the distinctive M16 noise. Consequently they would become even more vigilant. They had also started cutting communication wires and destroying radios, keeping just one to monitor the terr network

Dog once again proved his worth. Not only by his distinctive growl of 'enemy ahead', but also during the gruesome job of checking the shattered remains of the enemy. Most were lying in grotesque positions, caught at short range by the high-powered weapons and clearly dead. But one lay face down, with blood clearly showing the wound on his back. Dog approached him cautiously and growled, another tone altogether with an altogether different meaning.

Angus cleared the others in his group away from the dead terrorist and using a long tree branch cautiously pushed the man over onto his side, ducking down as he did so. The grenade the terr had been lying on exploded immediately, pelting the nearby surrounds with lethal shrapnel, but most of the blast absorbed by the terr's own body. If it hadn't been for Dog, Angus reflected, it could have had a deadly outcome. He, or one of his men, despite their experience and exposure to sudden death by booby trap would probably just casually flipped the terr over with a boot to the side. Deadly mayhem would have resulted. Angus reflected that perhaps they had become a little casual on their approach to the mission. Hidden grenades were common among murdered villagers back home in Rhodesia, particularly hidden under mutilated pregnant women and babies and all care was taken at all times. But this deep into enemy territory it was one out of the box of unpleasant reminders of the savagery of this war.

He glanced at the sun. About an hour left until sunset and they had come about twenty kilometres inside the border on their first day. He decided they would push on into the night, relying on Dog's sense of smell to detect campfires of further outposts. A few hours' sleep and start again at dawn. He used the radio to contact the nearest other Leopard units, which would pass the message onto their neighbours within range. During that day the others had reported in with varying results, from little or no contact to occasional heavy fighting. Terr deaths were estimated to have reached about the hundred level, while no friendly casualties had been reported. But a pattern was emerging of a corridor about five kilometres wide where contact had been virtually non-existent and stealthily dealt with.

Angus made another on-the-spot-decision, ordering the further outlying units to rendezvous the next day, probably about midday, he predicted, a further ten kilometres inland in the seemingly safer zone. A sterile five kilometre-wide exit zone would be more than enough, he reasoned, particularly with the SAS and RLI troops adding to their strength.

The rest of the evening past without further action, except for one small outpost which hadn't even bothered with sentries. Angus and his team used silent wet-work violence with knives and garrottes again to despatch the sleeping terrs, clustered around a dying campfire. By midday the whole team was back together, all with similar tales.

"Right," Angus told his men. "We concentrate on this corridor and take anything out which stands in our way. Short, sharp and lethal. We've all been there many times, keep as silent as possible." It was now just one and a half days until the planned attack on the terr base and they still had thirty kilometres to travel to be at the main site on time, set up and ready for the deadly action.

One day and most of the night was all it took, with the Leopards advancing with ultimate stealth down the designated corridor zone. They found little in the way of hostile outposts, which were quickly dealt with using ultimate surprise and sudden attack to wipe them out and the Leopards took up their designated positions, just short of the base. They bunched further together, built their camouflaged positions and waited. Daniel and Angus were joined together again, as the force split into three separate factions about two hundred metres apart. From then on, it was waiting time. It was now approaching the dawn of the fourth day, with the main attack scheduled for early morning, as most of the terrs would at that time hopefully bunched together having breakfast and getting ready to split into their training groups. Some, Angus knew, would also be preparing to head for the Rhodesian border to create havoc with their unadulterated savagery on both the black and white population in that land.

He grinned at Daniel. "Not long now, comrade," he whispered. Daniel just grunted in reply and did not shift his focus on the land ahead. He estimated they were in perfect position to fill their side of the job.

It began at 8am, with firstly an old DC3 droning back and then forward over the terrorist base, then closely followed by attack planes and bombers strafing the base and dropping cluster bombs and napalm, quickly reinforced by low-flying DC3's from which SAS and RLI made low-level parachute jumps, with the 'chutes barely having time to open before the troops made contact with the landing zone ground. But one fighter stayed on for a second pass. A terr must have got lucky with a SAM missile, because one of the fighter's wings disintegrated and the plane plummeted to the ground. There was no explosion, but its impact thumped through the sound of the troops now opening up with all weapons, mainly FAL-FNs. Angus had a clear view of the plane as it crashed and saw the pilot would have no chance, no chance at all of survival. First casualty, he thought for the friendlies. Among the terrs there was outright panic and slaughtered men lay in a bizarre pattern of burnt, bombed and shot mayhem.

The Rhodesian troops were laying down withering fire with everything they had and the scene resembled the scything of a cornfield. But many of terrorists had regrouped and were returning fire with their AK47s and even RPGs. They were continually mown down in groups, but had formed small enclaves in trenches from which they were offering vigorous defence. Angus saw two, then three, of the Rhodesians go down. Suddenly it seemed as if there was a turning point in the battle. Despite the carnage strewn around them, the defenders were returning vigorous fire and more Rhodesians were being hit.

Time for action, Angus decided. He waved 'forward' to the Leopards, who came in behind the SAS and RKI and patched up holes in their lines while some were helped out of fire-range, a couple badly wounded.

"We'll need urgent medivac," he shouted to Roger, the main radio man for this operation. Roger gave him a thumbs-up and immediately got on the radio. Angus summed up the situation. There was one particularly aggressive group of terrs who were well-covered in the trenches – from the frontal attack. But he could also see from the side angle, because of sloping ground away from them, they would be vulnerable. He gave the piercing whistle, which had a special meaning for the Leopards and easily carried above the guttural gunfire noise. The Leopards regrouped and followed Angus and Daniel around the perimeter of the clearing, to the north and then east. Concentrating on the main attacking force, the terrs were defending grimly with all their fire focused to their front.

Angus calculated, they were still three hundred metres away, too far for effective shooting. There was a further hundred metres of cover, so they powered through that, leaving them with just two hundred metres of cleared ground.

Just on shooting range, he judged, but not one hundred per cent efficient. Get to within one hundred and fifty and it would be all over. There were about forty terrs, he counted. It was a risk, but an educated risk.

At his shouted command "Go", the Leopards swarmed forward over the open ground, intending to drop and fire after just fifty metres of sprinting. But they opened fire as they ran, shooting from the hip, and saw immediate results as terrs started to fall, shot through the back.

But the new attack from the different direction had alerted the remaining terrs, some of whom turned to meet the new invasion.

One moment Angus and Daniel were running neck-to-neck, screaming with the rest of the men to release adrenalin and to add to the general mayhem. The SAS and RLI were still pouring fire into other strongholds with devastating effect.

The next moment Daniel cried out and went down and Angus immediately hit the ground and crawled to his best friend.

The rest of the Leopards carried on with the plan, as they had been trained to do. John and Jack would now resume leadership, so Angus and Daniel were left alone together as the battle raged ahead.

Angus could immediately see Daniel was in a bad way. He had been shot twice, once in the chest and again in the neck. It was the neck shot which troubled Angus the most, Bright arterial blood was pumping out at an alarming rate and Angus jammed his thumb into the open wound in an attempt to stem the flow. Daniel had been blown on his side and Angus saw with horror the pool of blood was still flooding. The bullet had passed right through and from the exit wound Daniel's life blood was flooding fast.

Daniel himself was fading fast, but still conscious, though his eyelids were being to flutter. Angus knew he would be in no pain, the shock to the nervous system would have seen to that.

Daniel managed to focus his eyes on Angus, who was now cradling his neck with one arm while he fumbled for an emergency field dressing. Incredibly, Daniel managed a ghost of a smile.

"We pushed it too far too often," he whispered, before seeming to lapse into a semi-conscious state. Angus could see the big man trying to fight the wound and once again his eyes opened, but they were growing glassy.

"Angus, brother...I love you man," he managed. Then he died in Angus' arms. Angus cried aloud with rage and pain. He and Daniel were blood brothers, they were closer than brothers and had been all their lives.

He gently lowered Daniel's head to the ground and closed the now-staring eyes. He bent further and kissed Daniel on the forehead with tears flowing unchecked down his face. He unwrapped the scarf from around his own neck and reverently covered Daniel's ravaged neck and face. He heard no sound from the still-raging battle. It was as if he and Daniel were together in an isolated dome.

Then the rage kicked in and Angus went berserk, filled with hate and the overwhelming need to avenge Daniel. Time, space lost all meaning as he sprinted towards the terr base, where at least twenty were still alive and firing, both at the first attackers and now at the now prone Leopards. He passed the Leopards, who as one rose and followed Angus, now at least thirty metres in front of them. Angus didn't bother ducking or weaving. He ran straight at the group, firing as he ran, changing magazines and screaming with incoherent rage.

He saw through the blind mist that had narrowed his vision to just the remaining terrs, seeing that he had killed at least five, but that wasn't enough. He reloaded the magazine again and kept firing until he was almost on them. He took a grenade from his webbing and threw it accurately into the midst of the remaining terrs with devastating effect.

He never felt the bullet that hit him. One moment he was running in blind fury, the next he was on the ground, the impact having thrown him backwards. The bullet had hit his chest, he knew and suddenly the rage flew from him, replaced by an almost surreal calm. He would be soon be joining Daniel, he thought, unaware that the firing had almost altogether ceased. There was none from the trench they had attacked, just forty dead and mutilated terrorists. The others seemed to have given up and were running at full speed away to the east, away from the main force of attackers, who were now helping them on their way with often deadly results.

Colonel Steve Archer, from the SAS, watched with awe. "That was the bravest thing I have ever seen," he said to his aide, who was urging the helicopter medivac in at full speed. "I hope to God that man survives."

The urgency in the calls saw four emergency helicopters arrive within minutes, settling in the safe landing zone and immediately gathering the most seriously wounded. Archer had despatched six men to gather in both Daniel and Angus...the rule was the Rhodesians always brought out their dead.

There were seventeen dead altogether and they were quickly loaded into one now-grossly overloaded chopper, which took off plane-like to build up speed to become airborne, which it gradually did and flew at a low altitude towards the Rhodesian base.

The wounded were treated far more gently, with emergency first aid administered by the medics as they were carefully loaded onto the remaining aircraft, the obviously spinal injuries first, laid carefully on their backs. Then the more serious cases. Of those Angus was one. He had lost a lot of blood, was unconscious but still, barely, alive. Nobody dared to object when Dog jumped on board and stood guard over his master.

At last it seemed, although the whole exercise had taken just a few minutes, the severely wounded were on board and the choppers took off at emergency speed for home and treatment at MASH-style portable hospitals set up at the base just inside the border, where doctors highly trained in dealing with battle trauma were already scrubbed and waiting. Treatment would be on the triage basis, the worst first.

The walking wounded would be helped out along the newly-created sterile corridor, with the choppers returning as they were able to collect the next most serious cases. Most would be home before the day's end while the rest would be collected as they made their way along the sixty kilometre trek to safety.

The chopper carrying the dead landed some distance from the hospital, mainly to spare the seriously wounded the further trauma of seeing the pile of their dead mates.

The first of the aircraft, carrying the most seriously wounded, including Angus, hovered briefly then flared and landed adjacent to the makeshift military hospital.

As they were unloaded the surgeons quickly assessed the most seriously hurt and those most likely to survive with immediate emergency treatment. Angus was among that group, who were rushed into the operating theatre and onto surgical gurneys.

Angus was still alive, just, but still unconscious and obviously struggling for breath. Blood was coming from his mouth but with just the odd bubble which was a heartening sign to the surgeons for it meant a lung had probably been nicked, rather than fully punctured. They went to work immediately, with the head chest-cutter in charge and were soon frantically working on Angus' chest wound. The bullet had passed through cleanly and thankfully missed the major organs. A centimetre or more to the right would have taken out the pancreas or liver and meant certain death.

"This one is saveable, God willing," the chess surgeon announced as he performed the urgent emergency surgery to stitch the nick in Angus's right lung. Now get him out of here ASAP," and turned his attention to other badly wounded soldiers.

Within an hour the choppers had the most serious cases on board, most with drips inserted, and were on their way to the nearest major hospital, in this case Bulawayo, where further emergency teams awaited.

The Brig, down from Salisbury for the mission, had been notified immediately about Daniel and Angus and suddenly with a shock remembered Sally Nkumo was an emergency nurse at the hospital. She would not know about either Daniel or Angus and he feared the possible consequences once Angus was rushed into the operating theatre.

He immediately called for his driver and within minutes was bustling through the emergency doors. He found Sally among those scrubbing up and gently led her to one side.

Sally took one look at the Brig's face, which was etched with compassion and anger and seemingly took the situation in with the quick glance.

"Daniel?" she softly inquired. The Brig looked at her eye-to-eye and nodded sadly.

"I'm truly sorry, Sister," he managed. "In the first wave of the Leopard attack. There was no hope, but he died instantly and in no pain." At least the second part was right, he reasoned with himself. He had heard about Angus' reaction.

Sally stifled a sob, but then collapsed into a chair and cried with all her soul. It tore at the Brig's heart. He, after all, was himself the man who had called Daniel with such urgency back into the war zone.

He stood impotently as Sally wept. There were no words of comfort, he once again realised. The Leopards had experienced a record run of few casualties over the two years since formation, but the Brig had far too many experiences in similar circumstances with suddenly heart-broken new widows and close family and knew there just were no words. The best he could do was to be there.

Sally eventually contained her sobs but still had tears falling freely as she finally looked to the Brig. "Angus?" she inquired fearfully.

The Brig looked her in the tear-swept eyes. "He's very seriously wounded, but will be here shortly," he quietly said. "I have arranged transport to get you home now to your family."

To his surprise and somewhat to his pleasure Sally straightened her shoulders and her bearing became more upright.

"No," she firmly said. "If Angie is coming here," she subconsciously used Matilda's pet name, though she had never even in teasing Angus used it to his face, "I must be here to help him."

The Brig marvelled at the courage Sally was demonstrating, the determination that would see her through this tragedy, although he knew eventually she would need serious time away from the hospital with her family. He also saw the Nkumo courage flowing into Sally's still grief-stricken face and realised it was a family trait, the same guts and determination Daniel had shown repeatedly over the years of his service to his country. His admiration for Sally grew enormously, as she stood unassisted then turned to the Brig.

"I thank you for delivering this terrible news, but now we have serious work to do at once," she announced, wiping the tears away and walking back into the ward, where the other staff had already been informed by the Brig's aide. They granted her a respectful distance, although three of her closest friends gently hugged her briefly as she passed them.

The Brig was struck by another urgent task he must perform immediately. Kate. Angus' pregnant wife must be told. He told his driver to pull out all stops on the way back to base, where he commandeered a chopper and flew straight to HillView. Better this way than a phone call, he reasoned.

The sound of the chopper landing just outside the farmhouse perimeter alerted Kate, who came rushing through the gate, instantly stopping as she saw the Brig alight alone. She went deathly pale and could have fainted had the Brig not rushed to her side and gathered her in his arms. She was, he judged, about six months along with pregnancy and the shock could induce terrible consequences.

"He's all right," he shouted above the chopper's noise as the pilot slowly silenced the engine.

Kate looked at him and the colour began returning to her face.

"He's all right, but badly wounded and is now on his way to the Bulawayo emergency department," he checked his watch. "Should be there shortly, I'm come to collect you."

Kate recovered much of her poise and looked directly into the Brig's eyes. "How badly is he hurt?" she demanded. It was a straight forward question requiring a straight forward answer.

"He was shot through the chest, but evacced to the border emergency hospital where they gave him the best help he could get in the circumstances, Almost certainly those surgeons saved his life, but he's now going to Bulawayo for further emergency treatment."

Kate closed her eyes for a moment, then said quietly, almost under her breath: "And Daniel?" The brig sadly shook his head. "He was killed," he broke the news as gently as possible, but Kate still reeled as if she had been slapped. "Oh my God...no," she whispered. "Not Daniel," as she instantly pictured the strapping Matabele, so full of life, so much a huge part in Angus' life...and now hers.

She wept anew as she allowed the Brig to shuffle her towards the helicopter. Matilda had also appeared and the Brig in a few words delivered the news to her. He knew of the intimate bond between the two. Matilda didn't waste time on words, but rushed inside and quickly returned with a valise of clothing for Kate. She also climbed aboard the helicopter and settled down, although she had never been, or intended to be, in one before.

"Angie is hurt, Kate needs me," she explained to the Brig, who just nodded and signalled the pilot to take off as the engines restarted with orders to land on the hospital's roof.

The trip, though quick, seemed as if the clock had stopped ticking as the minutes dragged by, with Matilda's broad arm around the weeping Kate's shoulders and her other hand alternatively softly stroking the girl's head and the bulge where Baby Dunrow was beginning life.

As the chopper landed on the roof, Matilda directly addressed Kate in the firmest terms. "Daniel is gone, there is nothing we can do about that," she firmly stated, although her own heart was breaking. "But Angus is alive and he doesn't want to see you blubbering when he wakes up."

Kate visibly pulled herself together. Matilda was of course right, but she still clung to the fervent hope that Angus *would* wake up. As a former emergency nurse she knew intimately the severity of chest wounds. Then a further thought struck her...she also must be strong for Sally. The Brig had told her Sally had refused to leave her post and insisted on being on the team which treated Angus.

They descended to the emergency department just as the badly wounded were wheeled in, Angus among the first arrivals. Kate rushed to his side. He was still unconscious, with drips feeding whole blood into him and swathed in bandages. His face was still covered in camouflage creams and there was still blood on his hands and arms. With horror, Kate realised the blood must be that of Daniel as she was bustled out of the way by the emergency team, which went straight to work.

She was also bustled out of the ward by Matilda, who simply stated: "There are some things a wife must not see. Angie is strong, he must live for you and the baby and somewhere deep in his warrior's mind he will know that," she said. She smiled with sympathy to Sally, who was about to assist, then led Kate down through the hospital doors and into the little park, where they sat on a shady bench.

Kate was still shaking, but had recovered some composure.

"Oh, he live alright...the bastard's too precious to me and the baby to lose now," she smiled tentatively to Matilda, who once again had draped her arm around Kate's shoulders. She realised with surprise Matilda had spoken the entire time in English, grammar-perfect English, not Sindabele. She knew, of course that Matilda spoke English but had always assumed it would be of the semi-pidgin that many of the house staff managed. Another arrogant belief shattered she thought irrelevantly and then her thoughts turned again.

"Poor Daniel...poor Sally," she said then began weeping again, but quietly, from deep within her soul. She remembered Daniel as the resplendent Best Man at the wedding, Sally the beautiful bridesmaid. "We must be strong for Sally, also."

Matilda nodded in silence and in silence they sat in the late afternoon waiting for news.

Chapter Twenty Two

Sally came through the hospital doors and crossed to the park bench and sat with Matilda and Kate.

"He's very badly hurt," she started, then stifled a sob. "Very badly...but he will be okay. Just time to heal is all he really needs. He's conscious and in recovery if you want to see him.

Kate rose at once, but was restrained by Matilda, who put her arm around Sally. Sally burst into tears. "Daniel," she cried, "Poor Daniel, he had just much to live for, so many dreams, him and Angus together."

Kate went to Sally's other side and also comforted her. Now she knew Angus would survive, she knew she must take time to help Sally. Practically, she said: "We'll take you home as soon as you are ready."

Sally nodded blindly through her tears. "Home," she said. "What is home without Daniel?"

Kate eventually rose, at a nod from Matilda and made her way to the recovery unit. Angus was pale from blood loss, with tubes attached to his body and wearing an oxygen mask. But his eyes were open, though focussed a hundred kilometres away. He was reliving, over and again, the terrible moment when he lost his best friend. Tears were sliding down his face. He could not come to terms with the horrible reality and for a moment Kate thought she may have lost him again to the stress of battle shock.

But as she sat quietly by his bedside and took his hand in both of hers, Angus' vision slowly came back to the present and he attempted a smile to Kate, a smile which wrenched her heart. "We lost Daniel and seventeen others," he mumbled through the oxygen mask..."Tell me it was worth it, Katey."

Kate shook her head and remained silent, as did Angus. The Brig had told her that follow-up reconnaissance had estimated the dead terrorist count in the several hundreds, perhaps more than a thousand, with God only knowing how many wounded were wandering lost and wounded in the bush. "They would be out there with severe oil leaks," he said with grim humour. The rule of thumb was two wounded for each confirmed death, so pandemonium would be raging on the hostile side of the Mozambique border.

But worth it? That was a question she could not face. She thought of the anguish on Sally's face, the grief and tears tearing her friend apart. And Angus himself, once so immortal, now not once but twice coming as close to death as any man could.

* * *

Daniel's body had been flown back to Bulayawo and then transported to his farm.

The funeral was traditional Ndebele, but with Christian overtures to acknowledge both sides of Daniel's own culture.

As was the custom, he was buried in the sitting position a distance from his kraal, facing north. Most of his clan group were present, quietly dignified in their best finery.

The Bishop of Salisbury himself, prevailed upon, by Jonathon, conducted the Christian part of the service, leading the hundreds of mourners in a caring and stirring ballad, *I Will Rise*, which included the phrase "No more sorrow, No more pain, I will rise again...on Eagles' wings". It was both strengthening and sorrowful.

Traditional Ndebele songs of praise followed, wishing the soul of Daniel a safe journey to the afterworld.

Daniel, Kate, Jonathon and Elizabeth were part of a large group of white mourners, including many Leopards, SAS and fellow farmers. Matilda kept close company with Sally, who had rallied with dignity, although tears flowed freely. Daniel had been buried in full Matabele dress of a warrior, with his many military medals, including the posthumously-awarded the Silver Cross of Rhodesia, for conspicuous gallantry.

Angus himself had been awarded Rhodesia's highest military award, the Grand Cross of Valour, only the second recipient thus far of the nation's recognition and appreciation.

He wore it, in full dress uniform, with the rest of his many military medals, although he stood stiffly and supported his body with a crutch made of the finest ebony.

He stood emotionless through the ceremony and only his immediate family and some veteran Leopards could feel his grief. Since returning to HillView shortly before the funerals he had been silent and withdrawn, sharing only with Kate his inner feelings.

"Daniel is gone," he had told Kate simply. "He was my brother and I shall always cherish him. For twenty seven years we were true friends and inside my heart he shall live forever." He'd smiled grimly. "But I will miss the bastard – oh how I will miss him."

Now, as the sun set, he and the rest of the family returned to Hillview. Angus removed his medals and uniform and packed them away. "That is the last time I will ever see them," he informed Kate. "I have given enough." It was a view shared by both the Brig and the Colonel who had given him the blunt choice: Retire or be retired. Both had treated Angus with enormous compassion for they too keenly felt the loss of Daniel as a loss to their army family.

Jonathon stayed on for a couple of days and eventually sought a private meeting with Angus in the study.

"I have sold Hillview," he bluntly told his son, who stared at him in disbelief. "For the past couple of years I have been divesting, quietly but thoroughly, from this country. We both know where we are headed. Life under Mugabe's rule will be untenable for both of us, Angus."

Angus began..."But it was you who always said the chicken-run was the coward's way out, we must stay and fight for our future and that of Rhodesia."

Jonathon smiled wryly: "Do you think for a moment Mugabe, when he inevitably becomes Prime Minister will allow us to live here in peace?" he said. Looking Angus straight in the eye, he continued: "I as Finance Minister, and member of the War Council which oversaw this terrible war for fifteen years now. And you – once the number one enemy of the terrorist movement...of course, now the Patriotic Front. Do you really believe they will leave us in peace?" he repeated.

"Mugabe makes public statements overseas, at Lancaster House in London, that black and white must bury the past and live together for the sake of the country.

"For God's sake, this country is now called Zimbabwe-Rhodesia and we even have a Black Prime Minister, Bishop Abdel Muzorewa, who Mugabe has already denounced as a white man's puppet.

"And we know Mugabe's true feelings about the Matebele. They may pretend to cuddle up together now, but mark my words, there will be terrible times ahead for those in Matabeleland."

He paused and sipped his whisky. Angus did the same, but kept his eyes firmly on his father, the enormity of what he had just heard beginning finally to sink in. HillView sold? Never, in his wildest imagination had he even contemplated that. He knew life would inevitably change, but the sale of the historic family farm had never shadowed the horizon of his future plans.

"So I have quietly sold HillView to an overseas corporation which believes it can deal with the future Government. Their terms are generous – you have many months to prepare for your future.

"Think of it Angus...do you want to bring your child up in such an uncertain future, knowing that every day you, Kate and the baby could be in mortal danger?

Angus blinked. He knew that as an absolute truth, as obvious as it should be, was no, he did not. "But what of Matilda, the servants, the labour?" he bought himself some thinking time.

Jonathon dismissed the distraction with a wave of his hand and Angus was reminded that his father had not risen to lofty heights in the Smith regime through charm along. He could be as ruthless as the best and always three moves ahead in the chess game of life.

"I discussed this with Matilda last night, having first sworn her to secrecy. She wished to return to her home village and has been substantially rewarded and I have established a trust fund so she will never lack for anything." He laughed for a moment. "God help the headman..Matilda will have the place reorganised in the blink of an eye. The house servant have also been given substantial payments and many also wish to return home to their kraals and family. The farm labourers, mostly, want to stay on, but each will receive a major bonus. No," he concluded. "That side of things is under control. It is now down to you and Kate to decide *your* future."

"Needless to say, you won't be short on for funds and will have direct access to a special account I have established for you in Switzerland. Now...as part of the divestment of assets here, I have also been investing elsewhere, particularly in the United Kingdom, Canada and Australia – mostly in Australia, which I believe has the most in common with Rhodesia. There is very little discrimination. I have bought a number of farms and also what we call ranches and they call stations. Take your pick, or you may wish to try your hand at something different. But I think within you there are close ties with farming and the land."

Jonathon looked directly into Angus' eyes, to the soul of the son whom he loved beyond normal filial feelings.

"Talk with Kate and think what is best for both her and for your child," he said softly. He recharged their whisky glasses and clinked his with Angus' "Today is over, tomorrow is your future, Angus, son."

The sat quietly together, in the soft leather armchairs with just the crackle of the fire in the huge fireplace keeping them company.

Angus let the sheer scale of the future sink in. His father was right, he knew deep within himself and for the first time in such a long time, it seemed, felt a glimmer of hope stir within him, like the embers of a flame being rekindled.

He just as suddenly make up his mind. With HillView gone, the future as uncertain as Jonathon so accurately painted it, it was time to leave, to join the multitudes of white Rhodesians already forming a mass exodus from their country.

"I would like to hear more about Australia," he told Jonathon, who visibly relaxed and began outlining his plans for the future in the new country.

* * *

Kate took the news with greater equanimity than he thought possible. "Your father is right, of course," she began, serenely settled into Angus's arms as they both gazed into the fire in the living room later that night. "Our future here is not one I would like to bring Baby Dunrow into. And Australia sounds wonderful. I like the sound of the baby beef venture in the south west of Western Australia. It sounds so tranquil."

Tranquil indeed, Angus agreed. And after the past few years in Rhodesia tranquillity had seldom been part of their lives together. Kate and the baby deserved a tranquil future, although he had no illusions about the hard work ahead – there was no labour force, no house servants, no Matilda to act as a nanny.

"Yes," he agreed with Kate. "And if life becomes too tranquil, there is also the cattle station in the Kimberley, in the north, to call upon. It's altogether a different country there from the south – wild, untamed, huge stations."

They nestled together, at peace at last. The final monumental decision had been reached. And they both agreed, that lingering would serve little purpose.

"One thing before we go, though," Angus smiled down at Kate, "one last swim in the pool. And we must say goodbye to Tom."

Chapter Twenty Three

Angus stood on the broad veranda of the new house they had built from local stone on the top of a hill overlooking the farm stretched out beneath them. At the rear, down a steep valley, the Blackwood River flowed year-round, a plentiful supply of marron, the delicious freshwater version of crayfish.

He'd established a marron farm on the property as well as a commercial trout hatchery, both ventures having proved surprisingly successful. He had leased out several hundred acres to a pine plantation company, with guaranteed annual income from their production.

Many of Jonathon's dire warnings over the future of Zimbabwe-Rhodesia had proved correct. Mugabe had won the election in a dubiously-conducted election and coerced the Matabele leader, Joshua Nkomo to become his deputy to show the world a united front and the fledgling new country, now just called Zimbabwe, had immediately been recognised by the United Nations.

But Mugabe's North-Korean trained Fifth Brigade had also gone beserk in Matabeleland, destroying entire villages and their occupants, with a death toll estimated by outside sources as up to 20,00 innocents. The tide of white emigration had become a flood as the remaining whites fled, often with little more than the $300 they were allowed to take with them. The white population had already dwindled from around 350,000 at its peak to about 50,000 with most of the skilled workers and professionals crossing the border post-haste into South Africa and from there to Australia, Canada, the UK and many other countries.

As Angus looked over the small fence, to keep the over-enthusiastic baby beef and sheep from the abundant garden, he again realised the value of Jonathon's actions in the last years of Rhodesia. They had indeed proved far-sighted...and accurate.

Angus' major challenge now was to keep the farm running like the well-oiled machine it had become, also with the regular trips to the Kimberley region in the far north of the State, 2500 km to the north, where the huge beef station produced high quality beasts for export to the hungry markets of Asia.

It was there, in the ruggedly beautiful terrain that he thrived in spending days on the saddle with his Aboriginal stockmen, checked on the cattle and joining the annual muster, backed by helicopters.

Initially the wuck-wucka beat of the choppers had brought terrible memories flooding back, but Angus had fought down the irrational fear and now enjoyed swooping into isolated waterholes, called billabongs, to fish for the prized barramundi.

He now watched Dog with a smile on his face. Dog had finally passed Australia's extremely strict quarantine regulations, which included six months in an isolation kennel and many blood tests. Now he had discovered sheep, which to his joy were well-accustomed to being ordered around by dogs, usually kelpies, and Dog helpfully rounded up a mob from time to time to drive them somewhere only he knew where. His enthusiasm was infectious and Angus often laughed outright.

Laughing, he reflected, laughing was now the norm on their beautiful south-west haven, which he had renamed HillView as much of it was dissected by the Darling Range, which ran all the way to the capital city of Perth, 250km to the north.

There had been many other changes for the better in the preceding four years, he thought, as he poured himself a sundowner gin and tonic. There were just two guns in the house, a rifle and a shotgun to deal with sick sheep or the pestilent rabbit and fox population.

And, best of all, Kate was thriving as mistress of her own house and occasional nurse-on-call at the Bridgetown Hospital, just twenty minutes drive away along the Blackwood River. She had also learned much about the animals they bred and farmed and could quite readily turn her hand to minor veterinary work.

And, best of all, she was pregnant again. The glow back in her features since their transition to the new life had taken on yet another new lease of life.

Angus looked down to the small fish pond, where a four and half year old boy was playing with Dog, who still towered over him and had adopted him as he previously had Kate. And Dog still slept on his own bed in the massive master bedroom.

"Daniel," he called to his son. "You'd better come and get cleaned up for dinner."

Daniel looked up at his father and smiled. He had inherited the best features from both his parents, the fire and enthusiasm from Angus, as well as the golden hair and the patience and wit from Kate.

Daniel laughed and ran to his Dad, faithfully followed by Dog, as Kate emerged from the house, her own non-alcoholic sundowner in hand. Angus put one arm around Kate and rested his hand on Daniel's head.

"This, my beautiful people, is where we're at," he said. He raised his glass. "To our future."

The end.

Printed in the United States
By Bookmasters